D1570403

THE OUTCAST OF LAZY S

Center Point
Large Print

**This Large Print Book carries the
Seal of Approval of N.A.V.H.**

THE OUTCAST OF LAZY S

Eli Colter

CENTER POINT PUBLISHING
THORNDIKE, MAINE

This Center Point Large Print edition
is published in the year 2008 by arrangement with
Golden West Literary Agency.

The text of this Large Print edition is unabridged. In other
aspects, this book may vary from the original edition.
Printed in the United States of America.
Set in 16-point Times New Roman type.

ISBN: 978-1-60285-149-8

Library of Congress Cataloging-in-Publication Data

Colter, Eli.
    The outcast of Lazy S / Eli Colter.--Center Point large print ed.
        p. cm.
    ISBN 978-1-60285-149-8 (lib. bdg. : alk. paper)
        1. Large type books. I. Title.

PS3505.O368O88 2008
813'.52--dc22

2007043542

1

FRANK SANDS leaned on Dutch Parkin's bar, covertly watching his son Karl, who stood at the far end of the room by the pool table talking to Jeudi Payne. Dutch Parkin was fond of saying that Jeudi was the best looking girl who ever set foot in a dance hall, that his saloon was the best house in the town of Sundown, that Sundown was the best town of its size on the John Day River, and that the John Day was the crookedest river in the state of Oregon. Since there was no other saloon and dance hall in Sundown, since there was no other town of the same size on the John Day River, and since the John Day is as crooked as a snake's back, he was probably right.

Frank Sands was thinking of that famous boast of Parkin's as he stood watching Karl talk to Jeudi. He agreed with Parkin in his opinion of Jeudi. She was little over five feet in height. She was slim and very dark, with a full curved mouth, curling black hair and enormous black eyes, eyes so genuinely black that one could scarcely distinguish the iris from the pupil. Standing there by the blond young Karl, who towered a foot and two inches above her head, she made an arresting picture. Her scarlet dress was a bright splash of flame. Her black hair was an ink blot thrown into sharp relief by Karl's tan and green plaid flannel shirt.

Sands admitted to himself that he didn't blame Karl for being attracted to Jeudi. He didn't blame any man

5

for that. He couldn't, being a man himself. All of the men who frequented Parkin's Place rendered Jeudi the distinction of being a law unto herself. Sands frowned and bit his lip and his dark deepset eyes were troubled with a look of uneasiness. Karl had been altogether too much interested in Jeudi for a long time. It was time something was being done about it.

Words of warning didn't always work, he acknowledged to himself reluctantly. Not when a man had got his head set on a girl as admittedly lovely as Jeudi Payne. And Karl was young, and his heart was free, his blood was red and his temper quick and hot. Sands involuntarily turned his head and glanced about the room.

The few men drinking at the bar and playing cards at the tables, or drowsing in chairs along the wall, were paying strict attention to their own business. A Sunday atmosphere of rest from labor hung over the room. Naturally, none of the men would be noticing Karl and Jeudi: Karl talking to Jeudi, or dancing with Jeudi, or laughing with Jeudi, had become too common a sight. Sands shifted from one foot to the other, impatiently, and his gaze swung back to the girl and his son. His deep eyes grew more troubled and brooding in his long tanned face, as he remained motionless, an empty whiskey glass between thumb and forefinger, staring at the two from under frowning brows.

Dutch Parkin, in the act of opening a bottle of whiskey for a waiting customer, glanced idly at the elder Sands, and his glance turned into a penetrating stare, as he caught the troubled expression on the big gaunt rancher's face.

"You got no call to be worryin' about them, Frank," he said quickly, meaningly, as the cork came out of the bottle's green glass neck with a pop, like an exclamation mark, supplying an emphatic end to his statement. "Judy's a good girl.' Everyone in Sundown insisted on shortening "Jeudi" to the more easily spoken "Judy."

Sands swung his gaze slowly to Parkin's face and the troubled look in his eyes receded as he studied the huge owner of Parkin's Place. Dutch Parkin was a mountain of a man, fully as tall as Frank Sands, and that was nearly two inches taller than Karl, and he weighed three hundred pounds even. He looked fat, but he had no flabby fat on him. He was as ugly as sin, with thin high brows over small green eyes, heavy cheeks flanking a great humped nose, and a pendulous mouth beneath a protuberant bushy mustache. The mustache was as straw yellow as his hair. Sands studied the huge man silently for a moment, then he spoke a word of agreement, almost reluctantly.

"Yes." Sands reached for the bottle beside him, lifted it and filled his empty glass. "You're right, Dutch. She's a good girl. That's just the trouble. She's too damned good a girl to be here in this place, associating with Mame and Tess."

Parkin shoved the newly opened bottle toward the man who was waiting for it, several feet down the bar,

7

along with a glass, then turned back to Sands, bristling in mild indignation.

"What's the matter with this place? I keep an orderly house, don't I? Anyway, you shouldn't worry about Judy, Frank. She can take care of herself along with anybody. Mame and Tess can't hurt her none. The more she knows the better she gits along in this world. The more she sees what happens to other people she watches out for herself better yet. I raised her up to all them tricks."

Sands made no reply, and Parkin turned abruptly to walk down along the bar and serve his waiting customer. Sands stared after him, then abruptly poured and swallowed his third glass of whiskey and started down the room toward the two young people standing by the pool table oblivious to everything else. As he walked, his disturbed gaze took in every line of the girl's finely chiseled face, the expression of her features, as she stood looking up at Karl, talking rapidly, as was her wont, one slender hand resting lightly on the table top.

Sands' frown increased to a scowl. The girl was in love with Karl, anyone with half an eye could see it. When a girl like that fell in love she didn't stop at anything. And Karl was half in love with her, too, although he apparently had not as yet realized the fact.

Sands increased his stride, unconsciously, with a sudden intolerable eagerness to get Karl out of there and give him a good talking to; but as Sands reached the center of the long room, past the open space always left for the dancers, a man lurched to his feet at the card table nearest Karl and Jeudi, swayed insecurely on his feet and leered at the girl.

He staggered a step or two toward her and raised his drunken voice.

"Judy," he ordered peremptorily, "you come dance with a fella. Here's Benny back again."

Benny Whitlock, the lean little roustabout who pounded the battered old piano without mercy and without music whenever the mood struck him, had just emerged from the small boarded-off room beyond the bar, and was draping his boneless figure upon the board bench which served as a piano stool. The man who stood swaying by the poker table gestured toward Benny as he spoke. He staggered across the intervening space and confronted Jeudi, roughly shoving Karl aside.

"Come on, Judy. Me'n you got to dance."

"Go back and sit down," Jeudi answered coldly. "You're drunk, Bark, and you know very well I never dance with any of you boys when you're in that condition. Go back and sit down till you sober up a little."

Barker Christy shook his sandy head. His slate gray eyes flared, and an ugly look flashed across his rather good looking face. He was built like a Greek statue, with something about him that fascinated most women and repelled most men. He drew his fine body upright and frowned in quick anger.

I ain't drunk. I'm just feeling good. Come on." He reached out a slim finely molded hand and gripped her arm with powerful fingers. "Come on, Judy."

"Let me alone," Jeudi commanded sharply. "I don't have to dance with any of you if I don't want to. Take your hand off my arm."

Christy frowned still more darkly, but he did not remove his gripping fingers. Karl drew close, his blond face expressionless, a warning in his blue eyes. Karl lacked the cut-to-pattern good looks that were Christy's pride, but his rugged features formed a face of striking power and high bred character. He addressed Christy in a lowered voice, but in a tone that should have warned any man.

"Take your hand down," he said. "If she doesn't want to dance with you, she doesn't have to. Hands off."

"You go to hell, will you?" Christy turned his leer on Karl, his every tone and expression belligerent in the extreme. "This is none of your business. Come on, Judy." He started to draw her forcibly toward the dance space.

Karl half lifted his hands, doubled into hard fists, and his blue eyes grew colder. "I'm warning you for the last time, Bark. Take your hands off Judy."

By this time every eye in the room had turned toward the little group, men at the bar halted in their drinking, card players let their games lie idly waiting, and Dutch Parkin stood stiffly alert at the end of the bar. Frank Sands had paused in his progress toward his son. The sudden tension of battle was in the air.

Barker Christy laughed loudly and shrugged in the

face of Karl's threatening attitude. He was a good five inches shorter than Karl and at least thirty pounds lighter, but he was muscular and tough, and what he lacked in weight and height he made up in pugnacity. His laugh echoed over the stillness of the room, disturbed the smoke wreaths in the air, and rolled into insolent defiant speech.

"Go jump in the John Day, will you? Dancing with us fellas is Judy's job. If I ask her to dance with me, she's goin' to do it. I suppose you think you can stop me."

Karl made no reply in words. He made one step toward Christy, his right hand lifted, rigid fingers outstretched, and the upright hand came down like a board, the lower edge of it striking a numbing blow on Christy's wrist, dashing the other man's hand from the girl's arm cleanly, shooting a twinge of sharp pain through the struck wrist. With a roar of fury, Christy whirled and swung at Karl.

The younger man was too quick for him. Karl's fist came up in a pile-driver blow, caught Christy neatly on the point of the chin and stretched him flat on the floor. A half dozen men rose to their feet, all over the room, and Dutch Parkin dashed around the end of the bar, to come to a halt at Karl's elbow. Christy lay spread-eagled, glaring up at Karl with murderous ferocity.

"You're the biggest fool in Grant county," Karl snapped at him. "If you haven't sense enough to realize that that kind of bullying doesn't do around

Judy, you'd better stay out of Parkin's Place. Next time I'll knock your thick head off your shoulders."

"And when he gits through doing that, I take the rest of you apart for exercise, py Gott!" Parkin assured him sourly. "Every time you come in here you git drunk and make a fool of yourself, yet. Better you git out of here and stay out if you can't behave yourself. Git up from there and go on back to your table, or I start on you right now. My hands is itching already, so you better move."

He hunched his great body forward in a lumbering threat, and Christy scrambled to his feet, glaring and muttering, then shambled back to his table. Parkin shot a sharp glance first at Karl, then at Jeudi, turned his back on them and walked back to the bar, a furious scowl on his heavy features, his green eyes shooting sparks. He was growing increasingly weary of having to quell Barker Christy's annoying disturbances. He stopped short once and looked back to where the disgruntled Bark sat slumped in a chair by the table from which he had risen.

"You don't git another drink tonight, either," he addressed Bark with curt finality. "You sober up and git out of here. Next time you come back maybe you can behave yourself."

Christy roused in his chair, his face mottled with the rushing blood of his baffled fury. "I ain't comin' back, damn you! I'm tired of the outfit that hangs around here. I'm sick of you and the whole damned country. I'm goin' to sell my ranch and go to Portland, where a fella can have a good time without a lot of yellow-bellied fools buttin' in all the time."

"I hope you do!" Parkin roared at him. "Good riddance of bad rubbish, yet. Git out right now. Git out before I throw you out."

Christy, obviously aware that he had gone too far in his defiance of Dutch Parkin, lumbered to his feet and lurched out of the room, grumbling and cursing, while half the men in the room watched him go with a great deal of relief. Parkin proceeded to his place behind the bar. Jeudi and Karl started to resume their interrupted conversation, and Frank Sands advanced to join them.

Karl looked up from the girl with a flashing smile of greeting for his father.

"Sorry to break up the meeting," Sands apologized, his somber eyes intent on the girl. "But Karl and I have to be getting along. It'll be daylight now before we can get home, and I've plenty to do tomorrow. Always have on Monday."

Jeudi lifted her delicate face and smiled at him, her black eyes sparkling. "What else did you teach him, Frank, besides knowing how to use a gun, and his fists, and his head?"

Sands grinned, then his face turned quickly sober. "Easy teaching, Judy. He took to guns like a frog takes to water, his fists were made for fighting and he was born using his head. Come along, son. It's going to be cold riding tonight."

Karl took casual leave of the girl and fell into step with his father. The room had settled back into its air

13

of undisturbed content. The men had resumed their card playing, drinking and talking. None of them was thinking of the little fuss raised by Barker Christy.

As Frank and Karl neared the door, another occupant of the room, toward the far end of the bar, suddenly aware of their departure, called after them.

"Hey there, Frank! Wait a minute."

Frank and Karl halted as one, and turned to look back. Pipe clamped in a corner of his mouth, from under the big oil lamp hanging from the ceiling over one of the poker tables, Tom Lucky rose hastily and hurried toward them.

"There's about a dozen head or more of your young stuff wandered down over the divide onto my place, Frank," he explained, halting as he reached the waiting rancher and his son. "We got 'em in a corral over in the south meadow, dragged 'em in with the fall pickup. If you don't want to bother with drivin' 'em back over the rims, I'd as soon buy 'em, if you care to sell."

Sands nodded. "Damned nuisance, Tom. What are they, yearlings?"

"Some of 'em," Lucky answered. "May be three or four two-year-olds."

"All right, Tom. Much obliged. I'll send Karl over right away.

"You better do that," Lucky advised. "The snow's going to be on us in damned short time."

"I'll send him tomorrow," Sands promised. "He can bring them back or not, as he sees fit. If he wants to

14

sell them rather than bother with 'em, he can price them to you."

Lucky struck a match to relight his pipe and turned to go back to his game. "All right, Frank. Goodnight. 'Night, Karl."

" 'Night, Tom," Karl returned heartily. Everybody liked earnest little Tom Lucky. "See you tomorrow." And Karl followed his father out of the room.

Outside the air was bell clear and so cold that some of the horses at the hitching rack were shivering. Karl slipped into the mackinaw he had taken down from a peg inside the saloon by the door, and buttoned it up to his ears.

"Brrrr, but it's cold!" he remarked, as Sands led their two mounts from the rack.

Sands had already buttoned his mackinaw high. He had not removed it when he went into Parkin's Place. "Yes, it's cold enough," he agreed, as he halted the horses and swung into the saddle on his own mount. "Tom's right. It'll snow within a couple of days, Karl. Well, let's get moving." He turned his horse toward the trail that led across the river and up the great bluff that reared behind Sundown, and Karl followed promptly.

The two horses they rode were noteworthy. The animals were identical in marking. Both had four white stockings, black manes and tails, white stars on their foreheads, and both were of the same build, big, rangy and powerful. They differed only in that one horse was dark brown and one was jet black. They were brothers. After night it would have been impossible to tell them apart unless they stood in a strong light. They started out at a swift walk, eager to be on the homeward journey, and the hard frozen ground rang like a steel drum under their big iron shoes. Their hoof beats banged hollowly on the wooden bridge as they crossed the swirling John Day River and approached the twisting trail that wound up the bluff.

The moonlight and starlight made the clear night light, cast the shadows of horses and riders on the trail. The sky was a dense blue infinitude, pricked with points of light where stars and planets winked. One lone cirrus cloud swept away from the moon to the south, like a comet's tail. Every least sound was magnified in the sharp air.

"Yes, it's going to snow, all right," Sands remarked. "You'd better hit for the Double Luck good and early." The Double Luck was Lucky's ranch, his brand was two swastikas side by side. "Better hit out first thing in the morning."

"Yeah." Karl answered absentmindedly. He was thinking of Jeudi Payne.

Sands sensed it, and he shifted restlessly in the saddle. "You'd better go slow with Judy, Karl," he said abruptly. "She's good enough, being brought up as she has been. But environment counts for more than a man thinks. And when a man marries—"

"Why, I've never even thought of marrying Judy," Karl interrupted, his wandering attention arrested instantly, and his voice was raised slightly in sheer

16

astonishment. "I've always liked her, but that's as far as it goes."

"I know you think it is," Sands replied grimly. "That's the time to put on the pedal, before you do get to thinking anything else. Many men like and admire the Judies of this world. But—they seldom marry them. Tragedy and unhappiness is the result when they do, nearly always. But what I started to say was this: when a man marries, the less he has to remember that stings and must be forgotten, the better off he is. It's too easy for things to happen in connection with girls like Judy, Karl. Judy is a child of storm. Be careful."

"Yes, sir," Karl replied dutifully. "I guess I know what you mean. Most of the fellows hang around Mame and Tess and Floss a lot. But there isn't any danger of me getting into any mess. Not that way— with Judy. There never has been, and there never will be."

"I hope you're right." Sands settled into his mackinaw, leaning forward to his horse's walk, as the animal half reared over a rocky hump in the trail. He looked up at the starlit sky, at the long veil of cloud which had now drifted quite clear of the moon. "But you can't see into things right ahead of you any more than you can reach up and touch that cloud trailing from the moon. I know. I know you *think* you aren't in any danger of getting into a mess with Judy, as you call it. But you are. The girl's in love with you, and she thinks she's got you hooked. I know you don't believe it, but I can see it. You go slow around Judy!"

Karl did not answer. He frowned, staring at his father's back, wondering what had sent his father off on that idea. He get into a low affair with Judy? He shrank at the thought. He didn't entertain any such intentions toward Judy. Although he was forced to admit that probably most of the fellows would, if they had a chance. He didn't like it because Frank had raised such a subject. He didn't know what to say.

"You heard me, Karl?" Frank's voice echoed against the face of the bluff they were climbing, bounding back in the clear cold air.

"Yes, sir. I—" Karl cleared his throat, as if that would make the words come out more easily. "I was trying to imagine what could have started you off on such an idea. It wasn't Bark Christy and his damned foolishness, was it? Bark's as harmless as a string-halted yearling. He's always blustering, but he hasn't the guts to raise any real disturbance for fear he'll get his pretty face spoiled. He makes a lot of noise, but he's a white livered coward."

"No, I wasn't thinking of Bark," Sands replied, rather sharply, turning in the saddle to glance backward into his son's vaguely distinguishable face. "And don't you be too sure of Bark, either. He's the kind to do plenty of mischief if he thinks he won't get caught. You keep out of arguments with Bark, if you know what's good for you. He's like a rat. You corner the damned sneak and he'll bite. I think you'd better stay away from Sundown for a while."

Karl assented silently, and with a vehement nod. But he said nothing. They came to another turn in the trail, and struck into the easier going of the homeward journey. Sands wisely forbore to press the subject. Karl had agreed to stay away from Sundown for a while, and in the meantime Jeudi might meet somebody else who would take her mind off Karl Sands. It was a slim hope, that, and it might materialize. But Sands realized how slim, knowing Karl.

Karl was one of those young men who carry about them that indefinable charm which wins men and women alike. His rugged blond face was tanned to a deep copper, and every line of it was fresh and young. His mouth had strength and firmness, supported by the power of the squared chin and jaw. Above his straight, slightly aquiline nose, his clear blue eyes burned with a daredevil reckless light, as though his life was half of laughter. Yet his eyes also reflected, ever alert and ready to flame, that quick temper of which everyone on the ranch including his father was always warning him.

The men of the Lazy S liked him and admired him unanimously, but they also were aware of that temper to the full and felt a concerted weariness about it. If it ever did fling Karl into trouble, they were agreed to a man, it would be nothing light. Karl did everything with all his might, with every ounce of his huge muscular body and every nerve of his clean quick brain. If he ever plunged himself into any fuss, it would be a bad one. Likeable as he was, upstanding and honorable as he was, that temper was gunpowder and none of them wanted to be the one to toss a match to it.

All of which Karl knew, and he was thinking of it, with some amusement, as he rode home beside his father. Let them believe what they wanted, he told himself, grinning in the cold moonlight. They didn't know that he had fully as much self control as he had temper. Karl had an idea that they never would realize that till opportunity should come to prove it. But— him get into trouble with a cad like Christy? He laughed aloud as he swung off his horse by the barn and began to loosen the saddle cinch.

"What are you laughing at?" Frank asked curiously.

And Karl laughed again, and answered with two words: "Bark Christy."

The two men slept a short shift that night, and were up before daylight. Sand's ranch, the Lazy S, was a large and prosperous cattle ranch on the north bank of the North Fork of the John Day River. The wide river, rushing down its rocky bed, afforded him an abundance of water. His ranch buildings huddled together on a ten acre flat. They occupied less than two acres of the ten, the rest of the land there being reserved for a feeding flat where the cattle were herded and fed during the severe months of the winter. During the spring and summer the animals grazed on the plateaus, slopes, and other scattered flats among the surrounding mountains.

The Lazy S lay at the very feet of the Blue Mountains. Round about it rose the great rearing eminences, separated by canyons and gullies of all lengths, widths and depths. The ranch house, a four-room building of unpainted lumber with a shake roof, contained a loft and was sealed inside with planed lumber. It stood within a few yards of the river, at the west end of the flat. North of it was the long bunkhouse, below it to the east stood the log barn, the pole and log corrals, the pig pens, and the stack yard with its great stacks of wheat, timothy and barley hay. Sands' timothy meadow, on another fiat across the river and down below the nearest bend, watered by a small creek running into the river, was his just pride, for not too many ranchers of the territory could boast a timothy meadow.

That morning, after the rather unpleasant evening in Sundown, Karl emerged from the cook shack after breakfast, filled his lungs with the crisp cold air and strode toward the barn for his horse. His footsteps slowed as he lifted his eyes to the south, where, in the first light of the early morning, the magnificent breaks of the John Day towered majestically against the sky. He loved the ranch, he loved the rugged country all about him, but he loved nothing of it so much as the towering breaks. He came slowly to a halt, gazing at them in never-ending awe for their magnitude.

From one thousand to three thousand feet they rose, so sheer that it would seem impossible for anything without wings to scale them. Their steep slopes rose from their feet in terraces, terraces varying in height from thirty to a hundred feet, to two hundred feet, every terrace rimmed by a straight-lying stratum of red volcanic rock that might be anywhere from twenty to a hundred feet in thickness. Terrace and terrace rose upon rim and rim, till the break ended in a high plateau that stretched away in the other direction. Scattered upon the slopes and juts of the terraces grew tall red-boled pines, always green and pungent in the mountain air. Karl caught his breath as he gazed at them. The breaks of the John Day.

Then he shook himself into action, and went at a long stride toward the barn. The air was positively biting. The nimbus sky was gray and threatening. Snow was imminent, no one could look at the sky and doubt it. He must lose no time about getting over to the Double Luck. As to whether he should bring the cattle back or not, he'd let the weather decide it. If the snow held off, he'd bring them back. If the snow struck before he could reach the Double Luck and start on the return trip, he'd sell the stuff to Tom.

He took his horse from the barn, and in less than twenty minutes he was on the way to the Double Luck. Lucky's ranch lay to the north, and to reach it Karl was compelled to go by a twisting and taxing trail, over mountains, through canyons, across the ridge of the divide and down on the other side. He took a steady horse-saving pace in the cold frosty morning, making the best time he could. But before he reached the Double Luck ranch the snow had begun to fall. He told Lucky, with a humorous grin, of the decision he had made, and ran an appraising eye over the young cattle Lucky had penned in the corral in his south meadow. There were eleven yearlings and four two-year-olds.

"Well, you can have the two-year-olds at fifty a head," Karl decided, "and the yearlings at thirty-five."

"Fair enough," Lucky replied, shaking the snow from his shoulders. "Come on in and I'll give you a check."

Check in his shirt pocket, Karl ate dinner with the Double Luck cowboys and started on the return journey. By the time he reached the divide the snow was coming down with fury, as near a real blizzard as it blows in the John Day territory where these ranches lay. The air was bitterly cold, and the small fine flakes of snow drove in Karl's face from the east, biting and stinging. When he started down on the side of the divide toward home, he could not see the trail ten feet ahead.

He crossed the little high flat that was a sun-baked inferno in the summer, Sago Lily Flat, now a stretch of unbroken white under several inches of snow, passed over Wildcat Ridge and proceeded along the ridge trail toward home.

He was making good headway through the storm, when a sound came on the wings of the wind that caused him to pull up his horse short and listen intently. The sound had been faint, but it had come clearly to his ears, too clearly to be mistaken. It was a high shrill scream, a woman's scream. Whether or not she had made any attempt to utter intelligible words, he could not tell. There might have been words in that cry, or it might have been merely a wild scream for help. Still, words were not necessary. There was something in the tone of the scream that caused Karl to stiffen in the saddle and strain his ears to catch the sound of it again.

Then the sound came again, and he located the direction from which it was borne to him. A man could have little sense of direction in that storm unless he knew the territory minutely, since the snow beat around him like a curtain of fog. But no cry could have carried against that wind for twenty feet, no matter how loudly it were uttered. The wind came steadily now from the northwest, the cry had come on the wind, carried with it; therefore it had come from the northwest.

Karl turned in his saddle and looked back into the face of the storm. Down that way was a canyon, Wildcat Canyon, falling away from Wildcat Ridge. The slope descending into the canyon was precipitous, rendered difficult of access because of boulders and pine thickets, but a man could get down into it even in a snow storm, if he had to do it. Karl sat rigid in his saddle, staring at the driving snow, and again the scream came to his ears, straight up out of Wildcat Canyon. For an instant his brain milled, imagining any number of wild possibilities. Some woman was lost, perhaps hurt, caught by the wild and swiftly rising storm. She must be a stranger, without any knowledge of the territory, with no hope of finding her way. If she were one of the women of the country, she must be hurt and unable to get home with her horse.

He swung out of the saddle to the ground, and started down from the ridge trail into Wildcat Canyon, leading his horse, with that terror laden scream ringing again faintly in his ears. The horse had been willing enough to go before, on the way home and with the storm almost at his back, but now, with the wind and snow in his face, his eyes and nostrils assailed by the flailing flakes, he objected forcefully. Karl was forced to fight with him every foot of the way, was forced to use every kind of persuasion, to keep the gelding traveling down the slope, around pine thickets, between boulders, toward the intermittent cry.

As he forged a slow progress through the storm and around numerous obstructions in his path, the cry continued to come at intervals, continually growing nearer. Karl made no attempt to answer, he knew the wind would whip the shout from his lips, deaden it under a hard-driven wall of sound-proof snow before it had gone a rod. For a moment he did contemplate firing into the air, to let her know that someone had heard her cry and was coming. His hand started automatically toward the heavy gun swinging at his thigh, then stopped. Reason told him that not even the sound of a revolver shot could carry against that gale.

He discarded all thought of trying to make any reassuring reply and bent all his efforts toward reaching her with all possible speed. He struggled onward toward the nearing cry, which was uttered at longer intervals now, as if she had despaired of being heard yet was unwilling to give up all hope entirely, yet it seemed to him that he must have been struggling around pine thickets and boulders for an hour, dragging the unwilling horse behind him, before he came finally to the canyon bed and heard the cry again, very close. In reality, he had not traveled more than an angling quarter of a mile before he had reached the woman whose screams he had heard.

Through the veil of white flakes, Karl descried the base of the opposite slope, not ten yards away, across the narrow width of the twisting half frozen creek. Almost directly across the creek from him two large boulders blanketed with snow leaned against each other beside a small tangle of pine thicket. Between boulders and thicket someone had thrown up hastily and carelessly a brush shelter. The cry had come from the brush shelter. The top of it was covered with snow, and the snow had beaten in a way at the opening which served as door into the shelter. Beyond the opening he could not see. Shelter, boulders and thicket were discernible, but dim, through the falling snow.

Karl left his horse standing, reins hanging, and made his way across the ice-edged creek, through the snow and smaller rocks to the opening into the shelter. There he paused, peering curiously into the interior. On the frozen ground, not ten feet beyond him, beside the ashes of a dead fire, a woman sat huddled into a thin blanket and a cotton quilt. The edge of the snow reached almost to the dead ashes beside her, where it had drifted during the last several hours.

She was young, younger than he, he judged, and she was a woman he had never seen before. She was no one who belonged in the country. Fine blond hair fell away from her frightened face, and the eyes that stared unbelievingly up at Karl were bluer than his own. She gasped out a sob of relief at sight of him, shoved back the blanket and quilt and sat erect.

"Oh!" she gasped. "What a miracle! I really didn't hope there'd be anybody around to hear me. But I—I couldn't die without—trying."

Karl hunched his tall body and stepped inside the lean-to. "How did you ever come to be here?" he demanded, raising his voice slightly that she might hear him above the wail of the storm. "Don't be afraid any more. You're all right, now I managed to find you. I was coming down the ridge trail just above here when I heard you scream. But how did you ever come to be here in the first place?"

The woman strove for calmness, relieved instantly at the sight of another human being, quite willing to believe him, that she was all right now since he had managed to find her. She answered the question promptly and lucidly.

"My husband and I have been camping here," she said. "Yesterday we were riding along the edge of one of these awful bluffs, the one just up back of this terrible canyon."

"You mean the ridge trail, along Wildcat Ridge," Karl interrupted. "The same trail I was coming down. It's tricky in some places, especially in bad weather, when the trail's frozen or muddy and slippery."

The woman shuddered. "It's terrible! I hate high places, and trails that are straight up one way and straight down the other. I was afraid all the way, but he wanted me to see this country. You know that place where the trail makes a bend around the shoulder of the mountain, and where the slope goes right straight down to the creek for several hundred feet?"

Karl nodded. "It's the worst spot on the trail. Why?"

"Because, I fell down there—or rather my horse fell with me on him."

Karl caught his breath. "You—fell down there? And didn't get killed? How did it ever happen?"

The girl shuddered again, and her expression, lifeless and drawn, turned ghastly beneath his gaze. "Oh, it was awful! Armor and I, that's my husband, stopped there to look at those mountains he called the breaks. They're beautiful, but they frighten me. I never saw such mountains."

Karl smiled, and saw his loved breaks in his mind's eye. "A couple of geologists told me there aren't any others quite like them in the world."

"I believe it! And Armor is rather mad about them. He wanted me to get a good look at them and that was the only place around here where we could get a clear view, he said. He knows this country well. He's come up here on his vacations lots of times. We stopped there and were looking at them, when his horse shied, bumped into mine and literally shoved him off the trail and off the edge of the bluff. I—oh, you don't know how awful it was! We turned over and over together, and I had a hundred visions of myself being crushed beneath my horse when we hit. It seemed to me we were falling so slow. I thought we'd never come to the bottom."

"You fell free of your horse?" Karl interrupted tensely.

"Almost." She nodded, her drawn face still deathly pale. "I guess he was all that saved me. He was killed. I really fell on top of him and bounced. I hit the ground so hard that it knocked me out, and when I came to again Armor was bending over me, feeling over me, to see if I was dead too. But I wasn't." She smiled wryly. "My right shoulder was wrenched pretty badly, and my right leg is broken just above the ankle. That's all."

"All!" Karl echoed, taking an impulsive step toward her. "My God, girl, that's plenty! When did this happen?"

"Late yesterday afternoon," the woman explained. "Wasn't that a horrible thing to happen on your honeymoon? Armor was just sick about it. He kept cursing himself for letting me ride so close to the edge. But he couldn't help it. He wasn't to blame in any way. His horse shied at a rattlesnake, and just pitched mine right out into the air."

"At a *rattlesnake!*" Karl repeated, a sudden look of suspicion flashing into his eyes.

The woman nodded. "Yes. It rattled, and scared Armor's horse. He heard it, that's how he knew what made his horse shy. I didn't hear it, but I never heard one anyway so I wouldn't have known what it was."

Karl nodded silently, staring at her. From the moment he had paused at the opening into the shelter, he had had a feeling that he had stumbled upon something ugly here in the canyon. He was growing more certain of it every instant. A rattlesnake, at this time of year. Small wonder that she hadn't heard it, since there couldn't have been a rattlesnake out of its hole anywhere. It didn't need a rattlesnake to make a man's horse plunge and rear, if that man knew how to dig his heel into a horse's flank and saw on the reins. But it would all appear very reasonable to the girl who knew nothing about rattlesnakes or about the country.

There was only one answer, and instinct and reason told Karl that in the same breath. The man had wanted to get rid of her, and he had spurred his horse into a plunge, forcing her horse to fall with her down that long drop onto the rocks below. It was a grisly thought, but Karl reminded himself that he had known something strange was here from the moment he had first looked in upon her.

"Where's he gone, your husband?" he asked, his voice harsh. "Didn't he do anything about your broken leg?"

The woman nodded eagerly. "Oh, yes, of course. He set it the best he could, and put splints on it. But it's hurt me so terribly that I could hardly stand it all night.

He went right in to town for a doctor. He said there was a town so close that he could be back within an hour or two. But he hasn't got back yet. And I used up all the fire wood he piled in here for me, and I couldn't walk to get any more. And it's been so long, and it began to snow, and I got so cold. I guess I just got so scared I didn't know what I was doing, and I started to scream for help."

"It's the luckiest thing you ever did," Karl told her grimly. "You'd have been frozen stiff before morning. It's nearly thirty below zero. Well, you can't wait here any longer for him. I've got to get you out of this to safety."

"But when he finally gets here, looking for me," the woman protested, sitting so erect that she winced with the pain in her wrenched shoulder and broken leg. "He won't know what to think. He—" She stumbled to silence, averting her gaze from Karl's penetrating eyes.

Karl all but said aloud, "He won't come," but he silenced the words on his tongue. He was not master enough of dissembling. She read the expression on his face, in his intense blue eyes.

"You think he won't come back—that he never intended to come back?" she asked evenly. "I—I've been trying not to think that. You have to tell me. I want to know. Why do you think that? How dare you?"

Karl's piercing gaze did not waver. He was cold with something other than the zero weather, the wind and the snow. He was filled with a cold fury for the low vileness of a man who could do such a thing.

"Answer me!" the woman commanded sharply, when he made no reply. "I know what you're thinking, that it's a terrible thing to say to me, or something of the sort. You can forget that. I've been thinking since morning that there was something horrible and frightening about it that I didn't know. I guess that's why I screamed. You have to tell me."

Karl took a deep breath. "Well, if I wanted to get rid of a man and didn't want to shoot him and be strung up for it, I could shove my horse into his on that ledge on Wildcat Trail and reasonably expect him to be dashed to death on the rocks below. And if that didn't work, and his leg was broken so he couldn't walk, I could ride away and leave him to freeze to death and know there wasn't one chance in a million of his ever coming out of it alive, in thirty below weather in a snow storm. His skeleton and the skeleton of his horse would be found in the spring when the snow went off, and it would be taken for granted that he had gone over the bluff, killed his horse, broken his leg and couldn't get to help."

The woman suppressed a little moan, and her blue eyes went sick. "Oh! You—you think he did *that?*"

"What do you think?"

"Oh, I don't know. I don't know what to think. I don't know why Armor doesn't come back."

"He won't come back," Karl said bluntly. "You say he knows this country. Are you sure of that?"

"Oh, yes!" The woman answered with pitiful eagerness. "He knows it like a book. I could tell that easily, from the way he talked and made his way about."

"Well—" Karl eyed her closely, as if wondering how rapidly her intelligence would encompass his insinuations. "There are no rattlesnakes out of the ground at this time of year, never. They've been in their holes for weeks. There is no town where one could get a doctor nearer than two days' ride away. A person with a broken leg is not helpless, even in this country—if he has a horse. He could have put you on his horse and taken you to a doctor. Didn't you think about that?"

The woman shuddered again, and nodded. "Yes. I— did think about it. But he said he could get a doctor within an hour or two—and I didn't know. Oh—I— what will I do?" She broke into stormy sobs, her courage shaken, now that her worst fears had been proved well grounded.

"You forget about him and what he tried to do to you. That's the first thing for you to do," Karl advised. The level, unexcited tone of his voice steadied her, and she looked up at him gratefully, as he went on talking. "My horse is just across the creek. I'll carry you across to him, and you can ride him home. I'll walk and lead him. I'll take you to my father's ranch, then we'll have a look at that broken leg. I think father can tell you whether it's all right or not. He's set several broken legs himself. Can you stand on your other foot all right if I help you up?"

The woman nodded, and he made his way farther

33

into the lean-to, picked her up in his arms and carried her outside, blanket, quilt and all. Outside, he lowered her gently to her uninjured foot, and she stood holding to his shoulder while he removed the quilt and blanket and surveyed her closely. She was very small and slight, scarcely larger than Jeudi Payne, he told himself, though he wondered why he should have thought of Jeudi Payne just then. This woman was manifestly from the city. The blanket, thin but ornate in design, the cotton quilt, her clothes, all were metropolitan articles. City was stamped clearly upon them, and upon her. In the lee of the boulders just inside the lean-to were a small camping kit and some agate ware dishes, a small hand ax and a very small supply of such food as a city dweller would carry into the hills.

There was not enough food to have lasted her two days, even had she lived through the freezing weather to consume it.

Karl gave the articles on the ground a mere observing glance, then gestured toward his horse waiting impatiently across the twisting ice-rimmed creek.

"I'll carry you across to the horse, then we'll get you ready to ride in," he told her. He picked her up again, spread the quilt and blanket over her as well as he could with her already in his arms, and started toward the waiting animal. He made his way slowly, through the thickly falling snow, taking infinite care lest he slip on the treacherous rocks.

He reached the horse finally, dropped the quilt and

blanket and lifted her carefully into the saddle. She cried out and winced as he shifted her broken left leg across the animal's back, but he settled her quickly into place and she held herself upright in the saddle, biting her lips to force back the tears.

Karl swathed the cotton quilt around her and tied it down securely with the thin ends of it, knotting it at her back and poking the other ends under the edge of the saddle. Then he started tearing the thin blanket into strips.

"I'm going to tie these strips around your hands and feet and face," he explained, working swiftly. "If I don't, you'll have frozen toes and fingers, not to speak of frozen ears and a frozen nose, before we get home."

He hurriedly bound the strips of blanket around her hands and feet, then swathed her small head in the wider strips, leaving only a little opening for her to breathe through, and another at her eyes.

The journey up the slope was not so difficult as the trip down had been. Both man and horse leaned to the ascent, skirting boulders and pine thickets and saving as much of strength for the long way home as they could save. On the ridge trail at last, they paused for a rest and a breath, struck again by the full force of the beating storm. It seemed to Karl that at least a year had passed since he had heard that cry of dark terror down in the canyon and had answered it, but in reality it was not more than an hour since he had started down the slope into Wildcat Canyon.

He turned his footsteps toward home, wondering

what his father would say when he arrived, thinking a jumble of wild chaotic thoughts. He remembered suddenly that the woman had not told him her name, that she had told him absolutely nothing about herself, save to describe what had happened to her there on the ridge. He found himself wondering what sort of person she was, where she came from, who her people were, and numerous other things a man might wonder in such a situation.

He set himself to the long tramp, making the best time he could make in the wind and snow, his one thought to reach the Lazy S with as little delay as possible. The sky had darkened, the early dusk of a winter day had fallen thick about them, when Karl at last led the tired horse up to the back porch of the house on the bank of the John Day. Frank had already lighted the lamp in the living room, and the yellow rays from the windows shone with a blur into the snow. Karl stepped close to the horse and looked up at the girl huddled in the saddle.

"You've been a brick!" he said warmly. But it's over. We're here, and in two minutes I'll have you in the house where it's warm, and have Groggs making you something hot to eat. We just got here in time. In another hour it would have been clean dark."

The woman mumbled a weary answer, and Karl made haste to take her down from off the horse's back. Walking carefully, mindful of the broken leg, he carried her up the steps, across the wide back porch, and kicked against the kitchen door. He heard his father moving about within the house, then crossing quickly to the door, to swing it open and stand peering out into the swiftly deepening night, the lamp held high in the doorway above his head. He started as he saw Karl standing there, and backed to make way for him.

"For God's sake what have you got there?" he asked blankly, staring at the muffled figure in Karl's arms.

"A woman," Karl replied succinctly, striding toward the living room, where Frank had a roaring fire going in the big cast-iron stove.

Frank closed the door quickly against the storm, and followed his son into the other room. He closed also the intervening door between kitchen and living room, then set the lamp down upon the table in the center of the room. Karl had already deposited the woman in a chair farthest from the stove, and Frank heard her voice for the first time, coming through the muffling folds of blanket around her head.

"Oh, do take me close to the stove. I'm so cold."

"I don't dare," Karl answered quickly, standing to his height, hunching and stretching the tired muscles in his shoulders. "Just because you *are* cold."

"Better leave the wrappings alone, too, son," Frank advised, standing with his back to the stove and eyeing the bundled woman intently.

"I was going to." Karl removed his heavy fur lined gloves and lightly began whipping the snow from the woman's swathings with his bare fingers.

"But why do I have to stay this way?" she asked

plaintively. Her words were barely distinguishable through the folds of cloth.

"She doesn't know much about this country," Karl half apologized to his father. Then he answered the woman's question. "So that your skin can get used to the change of atmosphere," he explained to her. "Your ears and fingers and face would hurt like the devil if you came in right out of the cold that way and exposed your skin to the warm air. If I hadn't bundled you up the best I could they'd have been frozen. You just sit still and let the warmth seep through, while I go out and put up my horse. This is my father, Mr. Frank Sands. He'll keep you company. When I come back we'll have a look at your broken leg." He turned to his father, giving him one long straight look. "I'll be back in a few minutes, Frank. There's a lot to tell."

Frank nodded silently. The woman did not speak. Karl put on his gloves again, turned and strode out of the room. The woman turned her head slightly, as she heard the sound of his departing footsteps and the closing door, but still she said nothing. Silence lay over the room, save for the crackling of the fire in the stove. The woman sat huddled in her chair, feeling the warmth of the room gradually permeating the blanket folds and the quilt wrapped around her. Even under those wrappings and the slow change of temperature they compelled, her skin began to tingle unpleasantly. Through the slit in the blanket folds which Karl had left for her to see through, she covertly studied the big gaunt man before the stove.

Sands stood motionless and silent, wondering what had happened, listening for his son's returning footsteps, glancing now and then at the bundled figure in the chair. It seemed to both of them that it was a long time they waited in the silence of the room, before they heard Karl come into the kitchen, stride briskly across the floor and open the door into the living room. He stepped inside the room, and paused, shaking the snow from his clothes, pulling off his gloves, and removing from his head the heavy fur lined cap which buckled from the furred ear-flaps under his chin.

"Well," he said cheerfully, "maybe we can unbundle you now. Ears begun to tingle yet?"

"They were tingling pretty badly a little while ago, my whole face was," the woman admitted. "Even my fingers and feet. But they're much better now."

"Then I expect it's all right to take the bundling off." Karl crossed the room toward her, unbuttoning his heavy mackinaw and laying it on a nearby chair with cap and gloves.

With deft fingers, stiffened a bit from the chill yet protected enough not to be rendered awkward, he removed the blanket strips from her head and hands, then from her feet. He pulled apart the quilt folds and shoved them back, leaving her sitting there with the quilt at her back and over her shoulders.

Sands studied her frankly as she emerged to his view, her slender figure, her fair and exquisitely formed face, her blond hair and clear blue eyes. Karl turned and faced his father.

"I found her in Wildcat Canyon," he explained simply. "Like that. With her leg broken just above the ankle, in a brush shelter, no fire, almost nothing to eat. She can tell you what she wants to."

She looked from one man to the other. "It's a long story, I think. And I didn't tell your son all."

"You'd better keep it for a while," Sands advised. "The first thing to do is to look at that broken leg. Who bandaged it for you? Karl?"

"Is he Karl?" She gestured toward Sands' son, and the elder man nodded. "We didn't have time for names, or much of anything, I guess." She shook her head, a look of infinite weariness passing over her face. "No. He didn't do it. My husband bandaged it and set it, last night before he went to get a doctor."

Sands raised his eyebrows inquiringly, but he made no remark about that. He crossed the room, knelt at her feet, and began carefully removing the bandages. She winced in pain several times, but she made no outcry. He removed the splints and examined the broken limb with cautious fingers, then without a word replaced the splints and bandages snugly.

"There was no need for a doctor," he said dryly. "No doctor could have set it better. All you have to do is exercise proper care and your leg will be as good as new." He brought a box from behind the stove, picked up an old cushion from a leather sofa situated just beyond the stove, and made a rest for her injured foot. Karl had stood silently by the stove, rubbing his hands together to restore full circulation, watching his father

40

with absorbed attention. When the broken leg was securely and comfortably supported on the improvised foot rest, Sands stood back and looked keenly down into the woman's face. "Is that better?"

"Ever so much better. It hardly hurts at all. Oh, you've been so awfully good, both of you. I don't know how I'll ever thank you."

"Just get well, and forget your nearly-tragic experience," Sands returned heartily. "I'll go out and tell Groggs to get you something hot."

"I've already told him," Karl interposed. "He ought to be in with it pretty soon. I'll get the table ready. I'm hungry enough to eat a bear raw. You two can talk."

The woman nodded, her eyes following him as he pushed the lamp to the far end of the table, and went to bring dishes and tableware from the kitchen. Then her gaze turned slowly to Sands.

"Yes." She nodded slowly, her face suddenly gone very white again. "I suppose it has to be said. The only trouble is, the most important part of things is left to us to guess. Only, sometimes, you can't help but guess right."

She told him exactly what she had told Karl, not omitting a thing either she or Karl had said to each other, while Karl quietly laid the table for their meal and Sands sat upright in his chair, watching her with a grim expressionless face. When she had finished, he nodded slowly, with reluctance in his face.

"Karl is quite right," he said evenly. "There can be

no least doubt of it. The man deliberately tried to kill you, failed, then decided to make a good job of it by abandoning you to the storm. He must have known a storm was coming. One look at the sky would have told him that. You might as well face it. But what's back of it?"

The woman shook her head. "I don't know. I met him—" She paused as the sound of heavy footsteps came from the rear of the house.

Groggs, the ranch cook, came into the room with a huge bowl of fried potatoes in one hand and a steaming coffee pot in the other. He had wrapped the bowl of potatoes in a stained dish towel. He set the coffee pot on the stove, unwrapped the bowl and placed it on the table. From a cavernous pocket he brought forth several slices of his good bread, and laid them on one of the plates Karl had put on the table. He looked neither to the right nor the left, and he spoke not a word till he had deposited all his offerings. Then he glanced at Sands.

"Will that be all right, boss?"

Sands nodded, smiling. "I think so, Groggs. There are some canned peaches in the kitchen. Karl can open some of them. Thanks, Groggs."

The stout burly cook nodded his muffler swathed head, and went out as silently as he had entered. Karl waved a hand toward the table.

"I'll move the table over beside you, so you can reach things," he told the woman. "If you're as hungry as I am, you won't want to waste time talking now."

He pushed the table across to her chair, so that the food was within easy reach, poured the coffee and pulled up a chair for himself. The woman thought to herself that she had never liked fried potatoes, they were so greasy, and the coffee looked black enough to hold up an egg. But hunger, a famous cook once said, is the best sauce. She found herself eating as eagerly as Karl, while Sands sat by the stove watching them, and smoking his pipe in silence.

The meal over, Karl rose to clear away the table, and the woman turned to speak to Sands. Her face was brightened, her body refreshed by the warmth and food, and a little vivacity had dispelled some of her listlessness.

"It's taking a long time to get around to things, isn't it?" She smiled, and settled more comfortably into her chair. "I started to tell you where I met Armor Fordham. I met him at a dance hall, in Portland."

Sands sat listening, while she rapidly recounted the things she felt it his due to know. She had gone to the dance hall without the consent of her parents, in fact against their express commands. She had become infatuated with Fordham, and had begun going about with him. Her father had seen her on the street with him, had taken a violent dislike to him, judging him to be a man of no worth and of vicious tendencies, had reproved her for her actions harshly and had forbidden her to have anything more to do with Fordham. She had told Fordham, and he had suggested that they run away and be married. Again, romance had seemed to be throwing a rosy veil around Fordham and his ways. She had consented. The two had gone across the interstate bridge that spans the Columbia river between Portland, Oregon, and Vancouver, Washington. At Vancouver they had been married. Then Fordham had suggested a honeymoon in the mountains, far away from Portland and the people she knew, up in the John Day country.

"I didn't know anything about this country at all," she finished. "But he made it sound so attractive, and the idea of coming to the mountains for a honeymoon—I suppose I thought that would be romantic, too. I didn't realize, as I do now, that it was a queer time of year to go into the mountains for a honeymoon. So—we came. And you know the rest. My parents are Mr. and Mrs. George Milne. I was Floria Milne, till I became Floria Fordham. I wish I was still Floria Milne—I wish I had listened to my father."

Sands glanced at Karl, who had cleared away the dishes and was sitting now by the table, listening. Then his gaze went back to Floria Milne Fordham. He smiled meagerly.

"We're always wanting to undo things after we're knee high," he said quietly. "And always finding that we can't. Well, there's nothing for you to do but stay here till you're able to walk again, and that's going to be several weeks. Maybe we can learn something about the fellow in the meantime, but don't depend on it. He's very likely gone completely out of the country, and won't come back. He hasn't any relatives up here.

There isn't a Fordham around here for a hundred miles. We've plenty of room for you, so you mustn't fret about inconveniencing anybody. The first thing for you to do now is get to bed and get yourself a good night's sleep. You can have my room, that one over there." He pointed toward a closed door just to the right of the big stove. "I'll sleep with Karl. Don't you think you'd better turn in? You must be worn out."

Floria found courage suddenly to ask a question that had been on the tip of her tongue a dozen times. "But—your wife? Will it be all right? Is she away somewhere?"

Sands smiled. "I've been so interested in your accident that I seem to have been neglectful. I have no wife. I'm a bachelor. Karl is my adopted son. You see, I had a bitter enemy once. He was a good man, but— oh, well, it doesn't matter. He hated me, without cause. His wife would have married me if he hadn't come along, and he never got over believing that she regretted me. She died when Karl was not quite two years old. Her husband was thrown from his horse and killed the same month, he was branding calves. Sad-dlehorn rammed into him. When he was dying he sent for me, and asked me to take Karl. I took him, and adopted him, and we both forgot long ago that he wasn't my own blood."

"But he's borrowed your blood." Floria smiled. "He even looks like you. I think that's as good as being your own son, isn't it?"

"Borrowed blood." Sands repeated the words

slowly, a strange expression on his face. His gaze went to Karl. "Have you?"

"It's a good idea," Karl returned with a chuckle. "I'll try to be worthy of it, Frank."

Sands rose briskly to his feet. "Well, Karl, I'll get the room ready and you can help Floria in."

Karl nodded, watching his father intently, as the elder man quitted the room. Like a blast of the wind howling outside, something swept across Karl Sands. For no reason on earth he had remembered Frank's premonition in Sundown only the night before, his queer certainty that something ugly was going to happen. And at the very hour in which Frank had been assailed by that feeling, this woman had been lying alone in the depths of Wildcat Canyon, cowed and frightened, abandoned to the storm. Karl rose as briskly as his father had done. When he spoke his voice was so curt as to be almost harsh.

"I'll carry you in," he addressed Floria. "We go to bed early here at the ranch."

THE NEXT MORNING, when Karl awoke and sat up in bed to find his father already up and dressing, the two of them looked at each other and thought of the same thing. "What are we going to tell the boys? Karl put the thought into words.

Frank shrugged. "What *can* you tell them—but the truth? However, it isn't necessary to tell them everything. I'll leave that to your own discretion. But no amount of beating around the bush is necessary. Half the boys on the ranch will be in love with her before the end of the week, and they won't give a damn where she came from. I'm half in love with her myself already."

Karl grinned, at what he thought a mere nonsensical pleasantry, threw back the covers and shivered in the blast of cold air that struck him. Ile glanced out the window to see that the storm was about blown out. Snow was still falling, lazily. From the window he could see the cook shack. A flat veil of smoke rose from the roof a few inches and bellied down to the ground with the snow. Groggs was up. None of the boys was in sight yet, and there was no sign of life at the bunkhouse. Plenty of time. Nobody about but Groggs. Karl grinned to himself at the thought of Soupy Groggs making any complications.

If Frank had said to Groggs, "go lie down and die," Groggs would have done it merely to please Frank. Soupy Groggs, with his lantern-jawed face, sharp tongue and magic hands (magic hands over a stove), had been with Sands before Karl had come to the Lazy S to become Frank's son: had been with Frank years before Frank's father had died. Groggs was more than cook at the Lazy S. He was an institution. There was no danger of Groggs' making any remark about Karl's strange arrival with the woman last night, nor of his expressing any opinion concerning the matter, of even allowing himself to have an opinion.

Karl leaped out of bed, reached for his clothes, and caught Frank's eye meaningly. "Floria is just Floria Milne, Frank. She was lost in the storm, went off the trail at Wildcat Ridge, killed her horse and broke her ankle. I happened along on the way back from Lucky's and found her and brought her in. That isn't exactly accurate, Frank, but it will do for Soupy Groggs."

Frank shook his head. "I think you'd better tell him as much of the truth as you can, Karl." He hitched up his trousers and tucked in his shirt tail snugly. "I don't like evasion, son, and it won't accomplish anything. I fear we haven't seen the end of this by any means, and to stick to the truth is the only way to protect yourself from unforseen circumstances." How sharply that was to come back to him in the black hours ahead, and to Karl.

"Oh, all right," Karl agreed. "I guess you're right. But we can't humiliate her by telling all the truth. We can't tell the boys exactly what happened—we've got to fudge somewhere, to keep her from feeling as low as the devil over it all."

"Maybe," Frank compromised. He stood, fully dressed, one hand on the doorknob. "Tell them what you have to and keep the rest to yourself, but don't lie about it."

There was no sound from Floria's room when Karl emerged into the dining room, and Frank had gone out to see how the stacks had weathered the storm. Karl slipped on his mackinaw, strapped his cap on and went

48

to find Soupy Groggs. The boys were up in the bunkhouse by now, and Groggs was busily beating a big bowl of pancake dough. He looked up as Karl came stamping into the cook shack, grinning cheerfully all over his broad perspiring face, the heat from the stove rendering the cook shack as hot as a summer day.

"Phew, but you've got it hot enough in here!" Karl unbuttoned his mackinaw and shoved back his cap.

"You always *say* that," Groggs returned imperturbably, ladling dough onto the hot griddle with an expert hand. "How's your girl this morning?"

"She's not my girl," Karl retorted. "She's Floria Fordham, from Portland. She and her horse went over the bluff into Wildcat Canyon. Killed the horse. Broke the girl's leg. She yelled and I found her. I couldn't do anything else but bring her in. That's all there is to it."

"Yeah?" Groggs deposited the bowl of batter on the rough board table and reached for his pancake turner. "What's she doin' up here like that all by herself anyway? Or wasn't she all by herself?"

"She was on her honeymoon. Her husband went in for a doctor when he found she'd broken her leg."

"Oh, yeah?" Groggs turned over a cake and cocked a scrutinizing eye at it. "Whyn't he take her in on his horse, like you did?"

"You answer it," Karl answered shortly. "His horse shied at a rattlesnake and shoved her off the bluff. When he found she wasn't dead, he set her leg neatly and went for a doctor. He could get one within an hour or two's ride. That's what he told her."

Groggs turned two more cakes, and raised a stare to Karl's face. "Rattlesnakes! Humpf! Well, he sure got a new way of doin' it, didn't he? Never heard of that stunt before. Not so bad—if it had worked. Couldn't string a man up for that." Groggs slapped five cakes on a plate and reached for the batter bowl. "What you gonna tell the boys?"

"What are you going to tell them?" Karl grinned.

Soupy Groggs snorted. "Hell! Tell 'em nothin'. None of their damned business. What do they care if you got a dozen girls in the house? Tell 'em you got comp'ny, that's all." He flourished his pancake turner threateningly. "Git out of here and let me cook, will yuh? The boys'll be in here to breakfast and not a damn thing done."

Karl laughed and turned toward the door. "All right, grouch. Frank and I'll be in here to breakfast in ten minutes, and you'd better have some real grub stacked up or you'll get fired. After breakfast you can fix a little something for Floria. She'll probably be pretty hungry this morning, and sight of your cheerful face will make her hungrier. Cook plenty."

"You go to hell, will yuh?" roared Groggs.

The door slammed behind Karl.

What ever Groggs may have believed, no man knew. Groggs was a master at keeping his mouth shut. When the boys came in to breakfast he told them casually that the boss had company, and fed them on fried potatoes and pancakes. The punchers were in good spirits. The stock was all in on the feeding flat, the work was down to a minimum for the next few months, and they didn't give a hang low many of the boss's friends descended unexpectedly on the Lazy S. They filled themselves on Soupy Groggs' excellent food and ambled out to the bunkhouse to play poker or read the mail order catalogue as soon as the cattle were fed. Bert Gray had brought in a whole gunny sack full of magazines from Sundown last week, so there wouldn't be much fighting for the catalogue.

After they had gone out, Groggs got together a breakfast for Floria. It consisted of pancakes, corn bread, canned greens, baked beans, with salt pork, and a huge bowlful of fried potatoes. Floria laughed in dismay at the heavy fare, but decided to dine lightly on the corn bread and beans, with a pancake as dessert. Groggs shook his head over anybody who couldn't digest his fried potatoes and black coffee. Floria filled the cup to the brim with thick cream, and still found the mixture too stout. In disgust, Groggs brewed her a pot of tea.

Frank was out with the boys, feeding the stock, but Karl sat across the table in the living room, keeping Floria company while she ate. When Groggs had laid out the meal, he started from the room, beckoning openly to Karl. Karl followed him into the kitchen, and Groggs stepped close to ask in a stage whisper:

"Does she know that she just sort of dropped in to visit you folks for a while?" Karl shook his head, and

Groggs advised anxiously, "Well, you better tell her. You better not lose no time about it, neither. Some of the boys might say something and she might spill the beans. No use makin' her feel bad when there ain't no use in it."

Karl grinned. "I guess not, Soupy. I'll tell her. Thanks."

Groggs grunted an unintelligible monosyllable and departed toward the cook shack. Still grinning to himself, Karl returned to the living room.

"What's funny?" Floria demanded, as he seated himself across the table from her.

"Soupy Groggs," Karl answered. "We decided to tell the boys only that you're company come to visit Frank and me, and Soupy was afraid you might spill the beans if I didn't warn you that you are just company."

Floria's smiling face sobered. She looked very fresh and fair sitting there in the cool morning light. Rest had restored the color to her cheeks, the contours of youth to her face. The drawn and haggard lines had all gone from her features. Her injured leg rested comfortably on a low chair Karl had padded for it with a quilt, and the pain in it was very slight.

"Soupy Groggs is a gentleman," she said warmly. "I think this ranch is about the nicest place in the world. And just to think, that it should have been you to find me."

"My luck!" Karl assured her. "We'll make you forget you ever had any unpleasant experience. There isn't much work on the ranch this time of year. All we've got to do for a good while is make you comfortable and entertain you. You wait! We'll have a high old time!"

He was a good prophet. The boys accepted Floria as a part of the household unquestioningly. If they had their own ideas and secret speculations, she knew nothing of the fact.

So Floria Milne Fordham came to the Lazy S, and only three men there knew that there was anything strange and bitter and ugly back of her coming. The boys knew she had sprained her ankle or something of the kind and had to lie or sit with her left leg propped up for several weeks. Frank brought out a mail order catalogue, and ordered a couple of changes of clothes for her so that she could be at home with herself and them. The leg healed perfectly, and she began to be up and around. Karl and Frank set themselves to seeing that she was entertained and kept happy. None of them ever mentioned Armor Fordham. Karl saw that Frank was increasingly gay in the woman's presence. He had no resentment for the fact. Rather, he was grateful for it. He wasn't in any hurry for either Frank or Floria to suspect his intense attraction to her. There was plenty of time for that, when things were settled about Fordham.

The worst of winter passed, spring was in the air and the snow was beginning to thaw on the south slopes, when Karl came in one evening to find Floria stirring up a batch of cookies. Ever since she had been able to walk about again, she had insisted on doing the cooking in the house for the three of them. Frank had been delighted. Frank liked a woman's cooking. Especially he liked cake and cookies, which Groggs hated to make. Groggs' specialties were fried potatoes—and pies. Frank was washing his hands at the bench by the kitchen door. He looked up with a smile as Karl ascended the porch steps, and followed his son into the kitchen, reaching for the towel that hung just inside the door.

"Somebody has to think of something," Floria said suddenly, pinching the edges of a cookie so that it looked like a small patty. Both men turned to look at her, wondering what she meant. She went on evenly, with a candor that amazed Frank and startled Karl. "I mean, about me. I appreciate all you've done for me, but I can't just go on staying here as a guest indefinitely. I don't know where I'm going, or what I can do. But I have to do something. I'd rather face it now and have it over. I suspect I need advice worse than anything else. I haven't any money. I must consider what to do next. My leg's quite well."

She laid two cookies in the pan beside her on the table, and turned to look at Frank. "Yet I can't go to work at anything much. My leg's not strong enough for that yet. I know what I'd like to do, but I haven't the courage."

"You mean to write home to your folks?" Frank asked quietly, hanging the towel upon its nail and coming to stand close to her. Karl followed him, silent and distressed. "But I wanted you to write them some time ago, and you wouldn't do it."

"There was no use then," Floria said quietly. She bent over the table, cutting out cookies methodically, talking as she worked. "I knew there was only one thing to do so far as they were concerned. I know Dad. The only hope for me ever to gain favor with them again was to wait a few months, till it had all blown over, and until they had begun to miss me enough to forgive me for running off the way I did. There's a chance that Dad might let me come back now, if I wrote and told him the truth and let him see how sorry I was for disobeying him. Oh, you know what I mean!"

"I think so," Frank agreed. "You mean that the fact that you'd been through such a harsh experience would soften him. And your absence, and your contrition over your behavior, would soften him more."

Floria nodded, and began laying the row of cut cookies rapidly in the pan. "Yes. The prodigal daughter, come home to eat humble pie. Dad's like that. Do you think I should?"

Frank thought the matter over for a moment, then nodded approval. "Yes. I believe that's the best thing you can do, Floria. I'm certain they'll be glad to have you back."

She returned his gaze, paling a little. He wondered why she should lose color, why that queer look came into her eyes. Karl wondered even more. But neither of them guessed what she was trying to maneuver. Here they were both face to face with the utmost guile, and neither man knew its countenance.

They were not such men as she had known, yet she was too wise to underestimate their shrewdness and intelligence. They had lived the life of the open range, where guile and feminine wiles were things out of story books, where the great towering mountains and canyons were changelessly constant, lifting windswept open faces to the skies, where men, women and life were all of the same pattern. She, being what she was, knew that they had failed to read her: knew by that very fact that she could win her way if she played her cards skillfully. She smiled into their puzzled eyes, the smile of an angel—an angel with two faces.

"But I have no money to take me home, Frank," she objected. "And they wouldn't have it to send me. They've always been poor. That was why I got to going to the dance halls. They couldn't afford to send me to shows and other kinds of places of entertainment. I think that's why Armor blinded me so easily. He hadn't much money, but he always had some, and he seemed to get it so easily. Blinded: yes, that's what I was." Her wide blue eyes appealed to Frank Sands for sympathy and understanding, and got it. "I was blinded by a fascinating rogue. But I'm not blinded any more. If he came back tomorrow and begged me to forgive him, I wouldn't have anything to do with him. I'm through with Armor. But I'm penniless. What am I to do?"

Frank laughed, shifting from one foot to the other. A bait as old as time, thrown to a gaunt bluff ranchman with a heart as open and rugged as the towering mountains around him. Karl's heart pounded. She had said she was through with Armor. There might be a chance for him now. She saw the flash in his eyes, but she gave no sign. She had known all along that she could have the son merely for the beckoning of her finger. She did not want the son. The money from, and the holdings of, the Lazy S belonged to the father. It was for the father she played. And Sands took the bait as readily and as unsuspectingly as she had shrewdly calculated that he would.

"Well, it seems the obvious thing for you to write home, Floria," he concluded. "I'll be glad to give you the money to go. The fare to Portland is only a few dollars. I'd be a poor kind of man if I couldn't help a girl that much, especially after she'd been through the trouble you have."

There was something in her eyes that did not escape Karl. It may be that his intense feeling made his sight keener. At least, he caught the queer little glint of hardness in her blue eyes, and for a moment he knew a sense of shock. It was a grim hardness, an expression of which he would not have believed the soft woman capable. It impressed him then, and he never forgot it. He was to see it again, and know how hard she could be. But the expression veiled, changed at Frank's words, and she smiled.

"You're a good man, Frank. I'll accept the money, because I know in what spirit it is offered. It will take courage to face my father's anger, but with you to stand by me, I'm not afraid. He'll be harsh. It isn't going to be easy to make peace with him, you know."

"It's never easy to right a mistake, Floria, never." The big gaunt ranchman seated himself by the table, watching her as she slipped the panful of cookies into the oven. "You don't have to eat crow, either. Simply tell them you've parted from Fordham, that he's gone you don't know where, and you'll never have anything to do with him again. Tell him that you're sorry to have caused him trouble and grief, and say that you want to come home. Don't say a thing about money. I'll give that to you, and it isn't a loan."

"No." Her chin went up, with a lift of bravery that touched Sands, called him to see how courageous she was. How well she knew the effect of that gesture. Some of the queer hardness came back into her eyes, was gone. "It couldn't be a loan, because I don't know when I'd ever be able to pay it back. It will have to be a gift—to life. Maybe life will bring it back to you from some other quarter."

"Listen, Floria." Frank leaned across the table, thinking how good and wise she was. Karl saw the dark brooding look on his father's face as the elder man went on speaking earnestly. "I'd spend ten times that much to bring you happiness and security. The gift is free, not to life, but to you—and nothing is expected in return. Karl, get Floria some paper and a pen, so she can write that letter right now and have the thing off her mind."

Karl obeyed silently, and the next day he rode down to the nearest post office to mail the letter.

Karl rode the several miles reluctantly, weighed by depression. He couldn't bear the thought that Floria might go away. If she went she would never come back. He would not let her go. If her father wrote that she might come home, Karl decided that he would beg her to stay on at the Lazy S, as Mrs. Karl Sands. After he made that decision he felt better and rode on to the post office whistling. How bitterly soon that cheerful whistle was to be drowned by a cry of despair and horror.

The next day he invited Floria to go for a ride along the ridges where the snow was melting away. She went willingly. If she caught the father she must humor the son. Karl sat the saddle easily, feeling the rush of life and delight in his veins. He rested his eyes on the towering breaks where the early spring sun was eating the snow away from the red rim rocks. He pointed out to her the beauties of the land he loved, the majesty of the mountains.

"Hear the pines whispering?" His voice was vibrant with the sheer surge of youth. "They always whisper. Gosh, look at the young flood, will you?" He pointed to a spring freshet rushing down a canyon to their right.

"Yes, it's beautiful country," Floria agreed. "Look: what's that over there on that rock? Why, it's a dog! What's a dog doing out here alone?"

"It isn't a dog," Karl corrected her. "It's a coyote. He's probably wondering what we're up to. They're curious beasts. Shall I drop him? He'd have a fine pelt this time of year."

Floria stared at the motionless coyote, her eyes alight with sudden excitement and pleased surprise. The animal stood like a statue, his pointed ears pricked forward, staring fixedly at the two human beings on their horses. Beyond him two tall pines swayed lightly in the wind and one great break rose upward toward the sky. A patch of snow between the red pine boles made a perfect background for the coyote's still body. Floria caught her breath.

"Oh! Really? Could you get him that far away? It's a shame to kill him. He's so pretty."

Karl smiled grimly. "We don't think they're so pretty when they begin raising hell with the calf crop in the spring. He's not far away. Sure I can get him. Little over a hundred yards, that's all."

He drew the thirty-eight from his holster and moved it out to arm's length, cocked it and pulled the trigger, all in one sliding lithe motion. The entire act was the smoothly executed act of the gunman born, had the woman known it. She only knew that his ease of movement fascinated her. She started slightly as the report rolled and echoed against the mountains' sides.

The coyote dropped and kicked, twisted from side to side twice, and lay still. Karl ejected the empty shell automatically and replaced it with a loaded one, and he had returned the gun to its holster, had turned his horse and started to ride toward the dead coyote after the pelt before Floria quite realized how quickly and expertly the thing had been done.

She stared after Karl with narrowed eyes. No ordinary young man this, she admitted to herself, to handle a gun with that dexterity and accuracy. Unconscious of her scrutiny, he rode on to the ledge where the animal lay, knelt, and with quick deft hands drew out his knife and skinned the carcass.

She exclaimed with pleasure over the excellence of the pelt when he brought it to her, and remarked emphatically on his artistry with a gun.

He laughed. "I've been able to shoot ever since I was old enough to carry a gun. There's a sort of trick to it, I guess. Eye, and hand, and knowing *when* to shoot. And practice. I'm always shooting at something."

But the woman had been strongly impressed, and she repeated the same sentiment when they returned to the ranch and showed Frank the pelt.

Frank agreed with her opinion, an odd little flash of uneasiness in his eyes. "Yes, Karl's an extraordinary shot. He's been considered the best shot in this country for years. Sometimes I almost wish he wasn't."

Floria made no further remarks about Karl's ability with a gun, but she thought plenty. Hers was a mind that followed all outlaw trends as a matter of instinct. She had already heard Frank and some of the boys speak of Karl's phenomenal ability with a six shooter, and she had also heard a good deal about Karl's hot temper. It was as natural as breathing for her to wonder what would happen if Karl should ever become enraged, and goaded into shooting at the man who had enraged him. He wouldn't miss the man, she was ready to wager that. It was also as natural as breathing for her to wish that, should Karl ever get into a gun fight of any kind, she might be on the ground to see the battle.

Could she have foreseen the kind of shooting that was to be done with her on the ground to witness it, she would have changed her wish with a terror of haste. Reflecting that wishing seldom brings any results, she went on into the house to supper. But she was still thinking of Karl's much-remarked temper.

So were the boys out in the bunkhouse. They were also talking about it.

"Cripes! Did you see Karl go up in the air when Dirty kicked at him last night?" Bert Gray was saying. Bert was always chattering about anything and everything that came into his head, and the boys seldom paid much attention to him. But this time he was discussing a subject of unfailing interest.

"He had a right to git mad," returned Tubby Lastover with spirit, and his round red face was flushed with instant indignation. "That damn Dirty's got speed, and he's one of the best horses on the ranch for endurance. But some of these days he's gonna kick once too often and Karl'll beat the hell out of him."

"Karl sure flies up too quick," Bert agreed, for perhaps the thousandth time. "But he ain't never hurt nobody yet."

"That ain't to say he never will," put in Clink Lafferty, and his long lean face was dour. "Tempers like that is hell, Bert. He's gonna git into trouble over it sure if he don't look out. And if he does, wowie! It'll be a peach!"

"Aw—change the record! Change the record!" Little Bass Todd horned into the conversation with an impatient exclamation. "He knows he's got a temper, and that's more'n half of it. He'll probably go through life without ever gittin' into a ruckus just to make you hombres all out liars. Besides, he's too stuck on that Floria right now to think of gettin' very mad about anything."

"Yeah?" retorted Lafferty. "What the hell you got to say about it? You're stuck on her yourself."

"So're you," grinned Todd.

"Sure I am. All of us is. But we got sense enough to know we got no chance with Karl hangin' around her like he does." Lafferty spat a wad of tobacco juice at a hole in the floor. "And lemme tell you I'd hate to be the fella that tried to butt in on any girl Karl was stuck on! He'd perforate me so fast I wouldn't have time to know what hit me. I bet you if anybody'd take that girl away from him he'd go so plumb loco he wouldn't know what he was doin'. And somebody'd git measured for a wooden overcoat."

"Well, dry up and git ready for supper," Bert Gray

63

advised. "Nobody's gonna try to take her away from him, you poor nut. Soupy's ringin' the bell, and we better be gettin' a move on."

"Just the same," Lafferty persisted, as he hurried to the wash pan, "I'd sure like to know what she thinks about it. She don't act as if she was none too gone on him."

Which was a thing that Karl had noticed himself, and wondered over a good deal more than Clink Lafferty had. He was still wondering about it rather uneasily when the answer to Floria's letter came. She took it into her room to read it to herself, and Karl and Frank sat in the living room in silence, waiting to hear what Milne had replied.

Then the door to Floria's room swung open, and she came out with the letter in her hand, unfolded. She laid the single sheet on the table in front of Frank. Karl was too highly agitated to note that the envelope which he had brought from the post office was too thick to have contained but a single sheet. He was too eager to know the contents of that letter to be thinking of anything else. He rose and looked over Frank's shoulder. He read:

Dear Floria: You wouldn't listen to what your mother told you. You would make your own bed, and now I'm afraid you'll have to lie in it. If you came home you would only make more trouble for all of us, so I think you better not come.

GEORGE MILNE.

Karl felt a surge of triumph. Now she wouldn't go away. He would not have let her go anyway, but this insured her staying even before he should tell her that he wanted her to be his wife. He had a pretty good idea that she knew he was going to ask her anyway. He looked up at her, tingling with eagerness.

The silence over the room was alive with the whirl of three people's thoughts.

Neither Frank nor Karl spoke. They remained motionless, staring at the two harsh sentences, and Floria waited, tense and ready. She joyed in the game; as all adventurers do, especially when they are sure of winning the trick of chance. It was Frank who spoke at last. He rose to his feet, and stood looking down at her from his gaunt height, his face stern, his dark eyes afire.

"I've wanted you to stay, Floria. I've almost prayed that something would happen, to keep you here. But I never prayed for anything like that to happen. The man is a narrow souled fool. I beg your pardon for speaking like that of your father, but—"

"I have no father!" Floria interrupted passionately. "I have no parents. I'm cut adrift. Oh, Frank—what shall I do?"

There was the supreme bait. Would he take that, too? She knew that he would. His voice rose angrily.

"You're right! What can the man be thinking of? To tell you that you must not come home, merely because you married the wrong man. But don't you care, Floria! You don't have to consider your parents again, if they are of a mind to treat you that way. Stay here. Stay here where you belong. The law will free you from Armor in short time. I'll see to that. Stay here and be my wife, and a mother to Karl. We both need you. Say you'll stay."

The rushing words ended on a high note, and Floria caught back the sob of relief that caught in her throat. She suppressed the smile of triumph that tugged at the corners of her red mouth. A mother to Karl! But what matter how ridiculous the man was? She had won the trick. She had gained the place as mistress of the Lazy S. Frank Sands's wife needn't lack for anything. He saw the expression in her face, and rounded the table in one lithe spring, placing both hands on her shoulders, looking eagerly down into her eyes.

"You're going to stay?"

She smiled up into his face. "Of course. I wanted to stay all the time. But I was beginning to be afraid you weren't going to ask me."

Karl stood rigid, staring at the woman in his father's arms, his face white, his eyes stricken. He was stunned, shocked to dumbness. This wasn't so. It couldn't be. She wasn't Frank's. She was his. He had found her, he had saved her from the storm. She was his—but she was going to marry Frank. Karl smothered a tortured gasp, turned on weighted feet, and stumbled blindly from the room.

It was characteristic of Frank Sands that he lost no time about making any move. Two days later he and

Floria left for Portland, well over two hundred miles down the Columbia River and a few miles up the Willamette River. He pulled strings and spent several dollars. Floria secured her freedom. She and Frank went across the Columbia to Vancouver, were married and returned to the ranch, all within a few weeks' time. The day they returned to the Lazy S, Groggs cooked a most extraordinary meal and the boys all indulged in a whooping celebration.

The next day the ranch settled into its ordinary routine. That was the day Frank sent Karl and Bert Gray over the divide to the Double Luck to fetch a small herd of saddle horses he had purchased from Tom Lucky. Sands always had a plenty of good saddle horses on his ranch. The country was hard on horses, and he did not want his men riding around on overworked mounts.

Karl and Bert set out immediately after breakfast, and the rest of the boys stood grouped around the bunkhouse door watching them ride off the flat.

Clink Lafferty frowned at the ranch house, where the smoke from Frank's kitchen fire was rising from the stove pipe. The hot sun of early summer was already high in the sky, pouring down on the flat and the mountains and the rushing river. Lafferty shook his head, shaded his eyes from the sun by tilting his hat farther forward, and turned his head to glance at Bass Todd.

"Damned if I like this any too well, Bass," he commented. "I never thought any man was going to take that girl away from Karl, and least of all did I ever reckon it could be the boss to do it! I'm scared there'll be hell to pay."

"Oh, you're always borrowing trouble," Todd grunted. "Don't be such a fool, Clink. Karl ain't goin' to kick up no fuss with his own father."

"He ain't really his own father," objected Lafferty. "You got to remember that, Bass. It reely ain't the same—it *does* make a difference."

"Oh, hell! You give me a pain!" Todd exploded. "He ain't raised no hell yet, has he?"

"Yeah, but they been away!" Lafferty pointed out. "They didn't lose no time goin' after they decided to git married, and all the time they been away he ain't had 'em before his eyes remindin' him of it. He was bad enough all the time they was gone, but he's been like a different man since they got back yesterday."

"Forget it!" Todd advised crisply. "You'd be lookin' for trouble if the whole country was as peace-lovin' as a gang of apostles."

"I reckon I'm agreein' with Laff, Bass," Kim Riceman put in, slowly. "The poor damn kid's hard hit. He's rid around the ranch like a lost dog ever since they been gone, and bet he ain't slept enough to satisfy a mosquito. It was bad enough for him just thinkin' about it, bein' so crazy about her like he was. But now they're back, it's goin' to be plumb hell for him for a few days, seein' 'em together right before his eyes, with her makin' over Frank all the time like she does. And it ain't goin' to be easy for him to close his eyes at night, thinkin' of her in there sleepin' with Frank. I tell you it's plain hell for him. I'm sorry for the kid."

"Yeah, so'm I," agreed Lafferty soberly. "Did yuh notice his eyes? God, I never seen a man look so miserable in all my born days. He'd be white as a corrpps, if he wasn't so damn sunburned. And the funny part of it is that Frank never even noticed nothin'.

"Oh, yes he did!" contradicted Riceman. "But he never thought of it bein' nothin' like that. He just thought Karl'd been workin' too hard. I heard him say so. Karl just laughed and said it'd take a lot of hard work to kill him off. But that damn woman, she knows what's the matter with him! You watch her. I don't care if she is the boss's wife, I don't like that woman, and I wouldn't trust her no further than I could throw a bull by the tail."

Lafferty looked at him quickly. "Hump! Funny! I don't like her none too well myself, now."

Bass Todd laughed, and there was an open tinge of malice in the sound. "Hell! You're just jealous because you couldn't git her. She's got a right pretty face, and I reckon any man'd want her. She's all right. Just kind of stuck on herself because she got a big man like Frank. They'll git along all right. You'll see. And Karl'll git over it. We all git over it. I've done got over several of 'em myself."

"Yeah, maybe," Lafferty retorted, unbelieving. "Just the same, I'm gonna keep an eye on that kid for a few days, till he sorta gits used to it. If he once gits to boilin' good inside there ain't no tellin' what he will do. Look at him now, look at the way he's ridin'!"

There was no need for the objurgation. They were all already watching Karl and Bert just passing out of sight into the trees. Karl was riding the black horse with the white stockings, Bounce, and he was slumped dejectedly in the saddle, as if he cared little whether he arrived anywhere or not. He was looking neither to the right nor to the left, but kept his eyes focused ahead squarely between Bounce's pointed ears.

He was thinking of the return of his father and Floria the day before, and he was very white under his tan, but for a far different reason than the men by the bunkhouse thought.

During the time Frank and Floria had been gone he had rather worn himself down with thinking, and his thoughts had reached an unexpected climax before the two newly married people had returned. Which climax was the sudden realization that his fancied love for Floria had been only a delusion, and that he was free from it. When the two had come back, he had met them with the inner exultation of realizing that there was nothing to hurt him in seeing them together. He had ridden the mountains and flats, as Riceman had said, alone and moody, thinking it out, and for the first time in his life he knew what it was to feel the sheer physical attraction of a woman like Floria.

He had lain awake most of the night before, after Frank and Floria had retired, exulting in his freedom from that purely physical infatuation, and he had ended by pitying Frank.

"Poor Frank!" he had said to himself. "That's just what got him, too. But he doesn't know it yet. I hope to God he never does. Maybe, if she tries hard enough to keep a hold over him, he never will know."

On that generous thought he had gone to sleep, and had awakened this morning. He slumped in the saddle, a seeming picture of dejection, simply because he was in a blissful daze of relaxation. He was colorless from lack of sleep.

"What's the matter, Karl?" Bert asked suddenly. "You look sort of on the hump this morning."

"Sleepy," Karl answered promptly, drawing himself briskly erect. "I'll snap out of it. Great morning, isn't it?"

"Yeah, sure is," Bert agreed, with the heartiness of relief. "Gonna be hot as hell, though."

He and Bert rode on at a steady pace, till they came to the ridge above Wildcat Canyon. He glanced at it with a smile of derision for himself, and rode on, his horse at Bert's flank. When they had passed the canyon, he turned to glance back, out of unadulterated delight in recalling the place where he had found her and in reminding himself that he was forever free of her fascination.

He saw smoke rising from Wildcat Canyon.

He pulled his horse quickly to a stop, a sudden frown on his features. Gray, hearing Bounce come to a halt, stopped his own mount and looked back to see

Karl gazing downward at the canyon and at the plume of rising smoke.

"Huh!" he ejaculated. "Now who the hell's got a fire down there, Karl? There wasn't any fire there when we came up the ridge. Wonder if we hadn't better look into it? Lucky and Chapman have been losing some young stuff, and they're on the lookout for rustlers. Did you know that?"

"Yes, Tom told me about it," Karl answered. "What the hell does anyone *want* a fire down there for? Looks funny, doesn't it?"

"It sure does," Gray agreed. "You better mosey down there and see what's doin'. That just might be one of those hombres that's trailin' a reckless loop. Go ahead. I'll wait here for yuh."

"I guess I'd better." Karl turned Bounce on the rocky trail. "It won't take long to see what he's doing there, wherever he is. I'll be back in a minute."

He nudged Bounce into a walk and went back down the trail, while Gray sat lounging in the saddle, waiting. Karl continued on till he reached the smoke. It rose from the very spot where the brush shelter had been. From where he had halted on the ridge, Karl could see a man moving about down below. He turned his horse to the slope and began an angling descent. The man might easily enough be one of the rustlers. Karl had no other thought just then. He had no premonition of impending disaster. He also had heard Lucky speak of missing cattle. The fire in the canyon was an irregular circumstance to say the least. The

72

man might be cleaning up evidence of some hurried branding job. It was well enough to be sure about it.

As Karl's horse started down the slope into the canyon, the man below stepped out from under the partial cover of a pine tree and stared up at him. Karl started involuntarily as he caught sight of the man's face. Even at that distance he was unmistakable. The man in the canyon was Barker Christy. Karl frowned to himself, and continued the descent. What was Barker Christy doing in Wildcat Canyon with a fire? Christy's ranch was down over the mountains on the other side of the John Day. He had never liked Christy. The man was too swaggering, too exasperatingly good looking, too insolently secure in his own fitness. An irritating person. But Karl had never thought of Christy as a rustler.

There was something queer about his presence in Wildcat Canyon, that was certain.

Karl brought his horse to a halt across the creek, and Christy stared at him with a scowl of open dislike.

"Hello, Bark," Karl said casually. "What the hell are you doing over here?" He glanced sharply about as he spoke. There was no evidence whatever of any branding having been done.

"None of your damned business," Christy returned curtly. "These mountains are open territory, ain't they?"

"Not to rustlers," Karl answered, quite as curtly. "And Lucky has been losing cattle. Just thought you might like to know that your presence here looks a little suspicious."

Christy continued to stare insolently, openly resenting Karl's intrusion. But back of the insolent stare there was a vague uneasiness, that Karl sensed rather than saw. Christy began to bluster. "There ain't nothing suspicious about you bein' here, is there?"

Karl shrugged. "I've legitimate-business here. There's a difference. You have no business here, and somebody might make it his business to find out what you're doing in Wildcat Canyon." That might force something out of Christy.

Rustling. Ugly accusation. Good for a rope around your neck in the cow country. Christy was afraid of a rope around his neck. He took a step toward the creek, as if he would impress Karl with his earnestness, coming a bit nearer to look intently into his face.

"See here, Karl: you keep it to yourself about me bein' here. I ain't rustlin' no man's cattle. I *have* got business here. I built me a little lean-to here between them boulders and the thicket last fall, and like a damn fool I went and left my hand ax and campin' kit here. I just dropped over to get 'em."

Karl stiffened in the saddle. Like a clarifying ray of light, the truth shot across his brain. A chill raced up his spine. Still, a man must not leap to conclusions on circumstantial evidence. He had to be sure. Eyes like blued steel, he leaned forward in the saddle and fixed his gaze on Barker Christy.

"There is no skeleton to find, Armor Fordham," he said, his voice a hard accusing blade that thrust deep into Christy's secret heart. "I came upon her and carried her in out of the storm."

Christy started violently, and his good looking face went utterly white. He winced as though the blade that pierced him had been sharp steel. His eyes protruded from his head. He tried to speak, choked over the words that stuck in his throat, and broke into incoherent babbling.

"You you're lyin'—damn yuh! No skeleton—you crazy? You—she—it—what the hell do you mean?"

"You know damned well what I mean!" Karl retorted sharply, cold with rage. "You low down coward! The thing you tried to do was the rottenest, dirtiest thing any man ever tried to do. You ought to be strung up for it, but you're out of reach of the law, and you know it. Nobody can prove that your real intent was to kill her. You thought you were infernally clever, but you weren't quite clever enough. Ninety-nine times out of a hundred you'd probably have succeeded, but this was the hundredth time. You failed. She didn't die."

"You're lyin'!" Christy interrupted frantically. "You just found something out—that—that you're tryin' to lay onto me. I don't know what you're talkin' about." His guilt was in his face, his fear was in his eyes, withering cowardly fear of what the consequences of his act might be.

"I carried her in, I tell you. But she's beyond your reach. The law freed her from you. She's married to another man." Karl's frosty gaze bored into Christy's frantic, terrorized face. "There's just one thing for you to do. Get out of this country, and get out quick. Unless you're looking for hot lead, keep out of this territory and away from the Lazy S. If I see you around here again, I'll kill you as I would a coyote. Get out! There isn't room in this country for both you and me."

Christy glared, and some of his terror subsided, to be superseded by a bland bravado. He was not a fool. Reason told him instantly that Karl had kept what he knew to himself, for the sake of Floria. Perhaps not another soul knew. He guessed shrewdly that it was Karl who had married Floria. He had been out of the country for months, he had not known of the local happenings. He was like a rat; cornered, he would bite. He was cornered now. His face twisted into a sneer.

"Maybe this country ain't big enough for both of us," he replied, with open threat in every word. "But I ain't the one who'll get out."

"Oh, yes you are!" Karl retorted coolly. "And you'd better make it snappy. Oh, no you don't!" Almost too swift for the eye to follow, his revolver had whipped from its holster and was covering Christy.

Christy had foolishly tried to draw his weapon on the best shot in the John Day, but before it could spit Karl had him covered. And Karl noted, as observant men do note seemingly unimportant things, that Christy was carrying a new gun. It was not the old forty-four caliber Colt he had carried for years, but a new Colt, of the caliber thirty-eight. Karl's intent blue eyes caught the light on the bright barrel of the new gun, his brain registered the fact of its replacing the old one and the size of its caliber, even as he snapped a sharp command at the desperate man facing him.

"Don't try that again. I'm not alone. Bert Gray is just up the ridge waiting for me. If you'd drop me he'd be down here on you before you could make a move to escape him. I'm warning you for your own good—you're so afraid of getting your neck stretched. Get out. That's all you have to do. I'm telling you for the last time, Bark. Get out!"

He thrust his gun into his holster, turned his horse and started back up the steep slope, between the boulders and the thickets, toward the trail. He had no fear that Christy would attempt to shoot him in the back. Christy would be afraid to make a move with Bert Gray waiting up there on the ridge. Karl rode up onto the trail and advanced toward Gray, and no sound followed him from the canyon below.

He wondered just what would be the process of Christy's mind, ridden by terror, shaken out of all its normal assurance by the knowledge that his attempt to commit a smoothly covered crime had been discovered. He felt certain of what Christy would do. He would get out. He was too afraid of getting his neck stretched to stay around. But Karl should have gone a little further in his reasoning. A man may be so driven by rage and fear that he will forget momentarily the greater fear of having his neck stretched by a rope. A man with the assurance to believe himself clever enough to plan and execute so nearly perfect a crime may be so driven by terror of having that attempt become public property that he will commit a greater crime to make certain that the traces of the vain attempt are wiped out forever. The first great error of Karl Sands' life was that he did not, in clear self defense, when Christy drew on him, shoot the man down in his tracks.

He had no such thought. He believed that he had threatened Christy harshly enough to scare him out of the country. He went on to meet Bert Gray confident that Christy would not hang around for any length of time. Gray grinned as he came up.

"Well, who is he, and what's he doing down there?" Gray asked.

"Some fellow who has no business there," Karl evaded. He couldn't tell Gray the whole truth. To tell him any of the truth would be to excite his curiosity unduly and might raise undesirable consequences. Better put Bert off the track. He did not think at the moment of Frank's warning always to fortify himself against future disastrous results by telling at least some of the truth. He thought of that later. Now he looked into Gray's eyes and added casually, "I don't believe you'd know who he is any more than I do."

Gray took that for what it seemed to be, and they rode on, for a little way.

"He's no rustler, though," Karl added further. "Just

78

some fellow passing through. Got a campfire down there, that's all."

"All right." Gray nodded, satisfied that the man was a stranger. "Let's fan 'er on the tail." And Bert Gray dismissed the stranger and his fire from his mind.

The two rode in silence for a short distance, and for each yard they went Karl grew more reluctant to continue the trip. He was in too much turmoil of mind to want to listen to Bert's usual meaningless chatter. More to the point, he wanted to make certain that Christy did move on. He suddenly drew rein, and Gray did the same, glancing at him in surprise.

"What's up now, Karl?"

"Nothing much, Bert." Karl pulled his mount to a dead stop. "But I don't feel like going on over to Lucky's right now. You can bring the horses on up as far as the divide alone, or get Fat Evers to help you. I'll meet you at the divide and help you herd 'em on home. I'll wait around. I just want to ride and think. You don't mind, do you?"

"Why, no. Sure not. I've knowed times myself when I wanted to be alone. See yuh later." But he looked oddly into Karl's eyes as he chirped to his horse and went on.

Karl ignored the look. It meant nothing, anyway, save that Gray was curious as to what subject so occupied Karl's thoughts. He forgot Bert Gray before the cowboy was well out of sight. He turned back down the trail, prodded his horse into a fast walk, and headed for the ridge above Wildcat Canyon. He noted as he neared the place that there was no more smoke rising from the deep gulch. But he rode on to the spot on the trail where he could see down into the canyon, simply to be certain.

Christy, with his shiny new gun, had gone. There was no sign of him anywhere. Karl sat his horse, motionless, staring down at the bed of the canyon, remembering the snow-driven day when he had heard Floria's scream from the brush shelter below. He found, almost to his surprise, that he had to force his mind to remember. He had all but forgotten the misery her marriage to Frank had caused him. There was no pain attendant upon thought of Floria any more.

He remembered that several months had passed since he had seen Jeudi. He wondered if she missed his coming. Frank had said she was half in love with him, and he wondered whether or not Frank was right. Somebody ought to take Jeudi out of there. Jeudi was fit enough for any man, thanks to that burly watch dog Parkin. He'd never let anything happen to her. But that was no place for Jeudi. Frank's fear that something was going to happen, with Jeudi as a pivotal point, was sheer nonsense. Karl told himself that he had proved that. And he really ought to go in and see Jeudi. He would, too. He hadn't promised Frank to stay away from her forever. He'd go in and see her sure Saturday night.

Deep in thought, Karl's sense of observance was caught suddenly by a movement at the edge of the flat. He straightened in his saddlc. A coyote loped out of cover and continued along the edge of the flat, next the trees. Karl spurred his horse after the pest. There was a decent bounty on a coyote's head, and the beasts had been bothering the cattle rather badly that year. Karl's hand flashed to his hip, and his gun leaped and spat lead and smoke. The shot missed, and Karl scowled. True, his horse was galloping and the coyote was running, but there was no excuse for missing it that way. Piqued by the inexcusable failure to drop the coyote at the first try, Karl spurred his horse to greater speed.

The coyote swerved toward cover, and Karl fired again. Again he missed. The coyote darted out of sight under the trees. Karl drew his horse down to a walk, reloading and holstering his gun, cursing in disgust. Temper and agitation had played hell with his accuracy, but that excuse did not ease his anger at himself. He could not remember when he had missed two shots in succession before. He would be ashamed to admit it to the boys. They would only laugh at him and refuse to believe it. That Karl Sands could fire twice at anything and miss both times? Not to be credited!

Disgruntled and wondering what was the matter with himself, Karl turned his horse about and rode on back across the flat. He dismissed the irritating coyote from his mind and recalled the much more pleasant subject of Jeudi.

He was still riding slowly along thinking of Jeudi, when he met Bert Gray just across the divide with the small drove of horses. He passed the time of day with

Fat Evers, who had helped Bert to bring the stock to the divide, Evers turned to go back to the Double Luck and Karl proceeded to the Lazy S with the horses. They arrived at the ranch late in the afternoon, and they were half way across the ten acre flat before Karl had the first inkling that Frank's fear of trouble had materialized at last.

3

BERT DREW his attention with the sharp exclamation: "Say, what the hell's up? Look there!"

He gestured toward three saddled horses standing by the big corral near the barn. Two of the Lazy S men were standing close by, talking excitedly. One of them, Kim Riceman, said something to the other, whirled and came running to meet Karl and Gray. Karl and Gray stared at each other, as Kim let down the bars of the big corral and motioned them to drive the small herd of horses in. He said nothing till the herd was corralled and the bars up, then he came rushing around the enclosure to where Karl and Bert Gray had reined their mounts to a halt. It was to Karl that he spoke. For the moment he ignored Gray.

"For God's sake, Karl, don't go into the house!" Riceman's voice was hard with repressed agitation. Karl started. Something in Riceman's manner chilled him. Riceman, a gaunt lean little man who said he had been born on a horse, was one of the regular crew of old hands who stayed on at the Lazy S year in and out.

His grizzled face was set under the thin short beard he always wore, his heavy brows bushed in a scowl. He lowered his voice abruptly. "Come into the barn, quick, before Frank finds out you're here. Bert, you and Todd can unsaddle yours and Karl's horses. I've got to see Karl."

Karl interrupted sharply, unable to control the wave of consternation that flooded him, the sure feeling that something hideous had happened. "Kim! Hold on there a minute. What the hell's happened?"

"Don't ask questions!" Riceman snapped. "Get off that horse and get into the barn. I can't believe it, remember that. She said it, but I can't believe it. There's something crazy about the whole horrible business. Move, man! Get into the barn. Bert, take care of those horses."

Karl swung out of the saddle and hurried into the barn at Riceman's heels. As he went, Riceman yelled at Todd, the other man standing in the yard, to help Bert with the two saddle horses. Todd nodded and walked to join Bert. Karl halted the moment he was well inside the barn door. He faced Riceman grimly, bracing himself for what was to come. Something horrible had swooped down upon the Lazy S. But what? "She said it, but I can't believe it." What had Riceman meant by such an exclamation? Karl thrust out a hand to grip the old cowboy's arm.

"Out with it!" he commanded sharply. "Whom do you mean by 'she'? Quick! *What* in hell's the matter?"

Riceman's gaze bored into him, grim and hard, penetrating. "It can't be," he muttered. "You aren't that good an actor. You *don't* know anything about it, do you?"

"How can I?" Karl snapped. "You'd better spill it before I choke it out of you. I'm asking for the third time—what the hell's come off here?"

Riceman stepped closer, his voice low, the words tumbling from his lips in a rush of bald explanation.

"It happened just after noon, as us boys was going back to work. Frank was in the house, talking to the missus. He was intending to come down to the horse pasture with Todd and me to cut out that bunch of three-year-olds. Todd and me had already started. Some man came sneaking up to the window of the ranch house. He—he—God, it's awful! He shot through the window—just twice. Shot first at Frank, and the shot done one of the crazy things that bullets sometimes do. The fellow shot at Frank from the side. Must have been aiming for his temple. The bullet went a little wide. It scored Frank's eyeballs and crashed through the bridge of his nose.

"Floria was standing within a few feet of him. As he plunged to the floor, the blood streaming from his face, she screamed and whirled to face the window. The fellow outside the open window, thinking he had got Frank, turned the gun on her. Todd and me heard the shots, heard her scream, where we was, almost down to the horse pasture. We come like a pair of bats outa hell, tearing to the house. Just in time to see the fellow racing out of sight. Couldn't get any kind of look at him—but we knew the horse.

"We rushed on into the house, and—my God, Karl, it's hard work, telling you this. We found the missus on the floor by Frank. Frank was writhing and groaning. She was unconscious."

"Stop it!" Karl cried wildly. "It's too horrible! It's a nightmare! It can't be true!"

"Wait—wait!" Riceman cut him short. "That isn't the worst. Frank—he was a terrible sight, his face all blood, that nasty hole torn through the bone of the bridge of his nose—blood everywhere. We got him up, Todd and me, and got him into a chair. We lifted the missus and put her on their bed. Frank sat humped over, gritting his teeth on a groan, holding his soppy handkerchief to his face. 'I can't see!' he kept saying, over and over. 'My God, boys: I can't see!' Just then the missus came to, and Frank sat up stiff as a board when he heard her calling to him. 'Frank, where are you?' she says. Just that. Then she saw him through the open doorway, sittin' there. 'Frank—it was Karl,' she says. Just like that. 'Frank, it was Karl!' Then she dropped back, unconscious again."

"You—you're mad!" Karl protested, stunned. "She accused me of such a preposterous, hideous thing? You're mad! You're out of your head. She couldn't have done such a thing."

"Wait—wait!" Riceman said again. His voice shook. "*That* isn't the worst. Frank got up from his chair, his face smeared with blood. Man, it was awful! *Awful!* What you could see of his face was dead white, fairly twisting with rage. 'By God, it can't be true!' he

85

says. 'It *can't* be! Karl! My son! He couldn't have done a thing like this.' Then his voice dropped to a queer ugly tone. 'But she said it. It must be so.' And *that's* the worst, Karl. Frank believes it. It's hell, but he does. He'd kill anybody else that said such a thing about you, but because she said it, he believes it."

Riceman faltered to a stop, his gaze on Karl's terrible stricken face. Every sickening, overwhelming emotion that rocked Karl showed on his pasty features. His eyes were staring, stark, half mad. Riceman went on hurriedly, as though he were fantic to be done with such a galling duty.

"We got him quieted down, finally, told him the doc was coming any minute, that we'd heard he was only over at the post office lookin' after Mrs. Hawly, and he'd better wait and see what the doc said about the missus. That was a lie, about the doc bein' at the post office. There ain't nothin' the matter with Mrs. Hawly. But we had to do something to get hold of Frank, so we made him believe the doc would be here right away. That was one lie that clicked, at that. Mort went to the Bar Ninety-nine, and the doc happened to be there—stopped there for dinner on his way in from Heppner. He come right back with Mort. He put Frank under ether to fix him up. I had to hold the damn can for him. I'm sick yet from the smell of it.

"He cleaned out the wound in Frank's nose, and took out a lot of little pieces of bone. Said there'd be a sort of sink there in Frank's face but he wouldn't be disfigured much. Only—the damned bullet went just close enough to score Frank's eyeballs, like I told you. Wonder it didn t rip 'em open, but it didn't. Just burned 'em. Just burned 'em enough to blind him for life. Doc said it was a wonder they wasn't torn out of his head."

Karl cried out as if a knife had been driven into him. "Blind! Frank blind? Good God, what a crazy sense of values *you* have, Kim! *That's* the worst, man! Frank— *blind.*" He buried his face in his hands, leaning against the wall of the barn, writhing as if it were he who had been shot and plunged into physical agony.

Riceman's voice stuck in his throat, his grizzled face was white and drawn under the thin short beard, but he drove himself on. "As for the missus, we don't know yet. I don't see how she can live, myself. But don't you go loco, too, Karl. Of course we know you never did it. We know why the missus must have thought you did, and it sure looks funny. But she made a mistake. It must have been some other fellow that looked like you for a minute, the way he was sitting in the saddle or something, and then she saw the horse. We all got a look at the horse just as he tore out of sight. But there's some crazy mistake all around. Nobody can believe it was you. Frank won't believe it either, once he gets over his first shock and cools down. You know what a hell of a temper he's got once it gets away from him. He'll cool down. He'll know she must have made a mistake.

"Besides, horse or no horse, you've got a perfect alibi. Bert can prove that you was with him after the horses every foot of the way. Lucky can prove that you come over there with Bert."

It was at that moment that Bert Gray and Bass Todd entered the barn. Todd had been telling Bert the whole ghastly happening, and the two came in just in time to hear Riceman's last words.

Gray paused, a queer startled look leaping into his deep-set eyes. His thin long face, with its hollow cheeks and jutting chin, turned slowly colorless. His blank, startled gaze swept over Karl dazedly, from head to foot. He looked as if someone had unexpectedly slapped him in the face. Karl shivered, knowing what was in Gray's mind. A peculiar, aghast silence fell over the tense little group of men just inside the barn door. Todd stared wonderingly. Riceman caught the look in Gray's eyes.

"What the hell's the matter with you, Bert?" he demanded, his voice raised in sudden sharpness. Something strained and desperate crept into Gray's blank eyes. Riceman caught his breath, and his voice shook a little. "Can't you speak, man? What's the matter? You can swear to that, can't you? That Karl was with you all the way? That he was with you when you talked to Lucky and got the herd?"

Bert licked his lips, as if they were dry with fever. His distended, startled eyes riveted on Karl's face. He shook his head slowly, automatically, as if it moved through no will of his own. The words came as reluctantly as though they had been torn from his throat.

"N-n-no. I—can't. He *wasn't* with me—all of the way."

"*What!*" Riceman thrust out a hand and gripped Gray's arm so hard that Gray winced. "What did you say? He *wasn't* with you all the way?" He turned a stunned gaze on Karl, then swung it back to Gray. "Well, why the hell wasn't he?"

"I—I don't know." Gray's eyes clung to Karl's stony face, as if begging him to say something to set this mad twist of things right. "All I know is that, as we was climbin' the ridge, we saw a fire—some smoke, I mean—we saw it comin' out of Wildcat Canyon. We—we wondered if the fella that had the fire could have any connection with—with them rustlers Chapman and Lucky was complainin' about. Karl went back to find out. He come back and told me the fella was a stranger—just passin' through, Karl said. He didn't know him. He—we rode on a little further, and Karl asked me to go on to the Double Luck and leave him there. He—he said he just wanted to be alone. I didn't see him no more till I got back to the divide with the herd."

Stunned surprise held them all in silence for another long moment. Riceman passed his hand before his eyes and shook his head violently, as if to clear his sight. He looked from one to the other, apparently seeing neither of them, shifted his gaze to Bert, to Karl, back to Bert, and then to Karl again. "By God, that ain't so good," he said slowly, "but it really ain't anything against Karl. His gun'll prove that. If he'd fired at anything,—well, there'd have been a couple of shots fired, that's all. We'll settle that little thing right here. Let's have your gun, Karl!"

Karl stood motionless, frozen into immobility. He was as unable to move as a dead man. He felt his flesh go cold, all over his body, numb to the bone. His heart pounded till the sound was like thunder in his ears. The others looked at him blankly, puzzled, waiting for him to make some move. He simply stood there, scarcely breathing, staring wide-eyed into Riceman's face.

Slowly something like a veil of fog passed over Riceman's features, leaving a queer film of hardness as it passed. His eyes narrowed, and a little stony glitter lighted in their depths.

What in hell's the matter, Karl?" he demanded. "Didn't you hear me ask you to hand over your gun?" Karl remained as he was, staring as if he had not heard. With a sharp exclamation of impatience, Riceman reached out and jerked Karl's gun from its holster.

He broke it and threw open the cylinder. The cylinder was full. He ejected the six loaded shells, raised the gun toward the light streaming through the doorway and peered into the cylinder. At the lower rim of two of the cartridge chambers were two little rings of powder smudge. Riceman slowly returned the shells and closed the gun.

"It's been fired twice," he said. His eyes were incredulous, but his voice was hard.

Cold ugly silence settled over the barn's interior. Karl's staring gaze dropped to the gun hanging in Riceman's hand. Yes, it had been fired twice. Two shots had been fired at Frank and Floria, only two. Karl had fired twice at a coyote, and missed. He had no dead coyote to prove it. Empty shells from his gun on the fiat would prove nothing. Empty shells from his gun were scattered all over the mountains. Two shots at a coyote, and missed. They would not believe it, these men standing here, staring at the accusing gun Riceman held. Karl, the crack shot of the John Day. But he had to say it. He had to tell the truth. It was then he remembered what Frank had said about telling the truth.

"I fired at a coyote, up on Sago Lily Flat," he said hoarsely. "Missed both times."

Riceman stared and shook his head. "You fired twice at a coyote no farther away from you than across Sago Lily Flat, and missed both times? God Karl! Can't you do better than that?"

"It's the truth!" Karl cried desperately. "He was running, and my horse was galloping. I—I—was upset. I just missed."

"The bullets," Todd said into the silence, harshly. "The bullets that were fired at Frank and the missus— me and Lafferty dug 'em out of the wall. They wasn't flattened much. They was thirty-eights."

Karl wanted to cry aloud, to shout in just rebellion his indignant protest at the trap that was closing about him. Could the malignant fates think of anything more? Thirty-eights. He was the only man in the county who carried a thirty-eight. The rest of the boys carried forty-fives and forty-fours. A couple of the boys on the Cross Crooked K carried old forty-ones. But no one else owned a gun with so small a caliber as the thirty-eight Riceman held in his hand, the gun from Karl's holster.

Then Karl did cry out, remembering. "But I know who it was! It was Bark Christy! It was Bark Christy in Wildcat Canyon. I didn't see any need of telling Bert—I had my reasons. I'm not telling them unless I have to."

"Bark carries a forty-four," said Riceman coldly.

"He has a new one, he had it there today," Karl argued feverishly. "A brand new thirty-eight Colt. He tried to draw it on me."

"You're getting wilder and wilder, Karl," Todd cut in. "Bark left the country months ago. I heard it in Sundown, everybody knows it. He simply up and left everything and got out. He ain't been heard of since."

"Well, he's come back!" Karl insisted. "He was there in Wildcat Canyon today."

Bert Gray shook his head. "If it'd been Bark you'd have told me when you come up from the canyon."

Something electric passed between Riceman, Gray and Todd, the first sure conviction of guilt in Karl, the first positive suspicion that he, reluctant as they were to admit it, had done the thing none of them had believed he could do. Riceman stepped closer, his eyes hard, his voice cold.

"I told you we all saw the horse, but we were still hanging onto our belief in you. We might have known, then. It was the horse you were riding today. The black horse with the four white feet."

"It couldn't have been!" Karl blazed. "I had him! Christy must have caught up Ball, he was running loose out that way. But he couldn't have had Bounce. I was riding him."

"Just so," agreed Riceman coldly. "You were riding him. And it was Bounce we saw disappearing into the trees. Don't you suppose we could have seen the brown of Ball's coat?"

"Just disappearing into the shadows he might have looked as black as Bounce," Karl argued in a fury of self defense.

"There's one chance left," Riceman returned. "What were you doing during the time Bert went on over to the Double Luck for the herd? If you've any reasonable kind of alibi, now's the time to say so. And talk fast!"

Karl thought swiftly in that blind moment. The truth now, and all of it. Nothing could be kept back now. He broke into swift terse sentences. "It begins with Floria. Her husband brought her up here to kill her. He tried to do it by shoving his horse against hers. Knocking her off Wildcat Ridge. It killed her horse. Broke her leg. He set her leg, told her he was going for a doctor, and left her to freeze to death. I found her in Wildcat Gulch and brought her home. The man she married was Bark Christy under an alias, called himself Armor

93

Fordham. He came back here to be sure she'd died there in the gulch. That's what he was doing today. I told him I'd saved her. Can't you see what happened? He went wild, caught up Ball, rode down here and tried to kill her and Frank."

Riceman shook his head. "Too thin, Karl. The part about the missus may be true, I suppose it is. But the rest—it don't go down."

"It has to go down!" Karl flared at him. "It's the truth!"

Riceman laughed, a short, sneering, ugly sound. He flashed a look at Todd. The two started to put the desperate Karl through a harsh third degree, then the rest of the men came in. Karl's story was rehashed, to unbelieving ears and deriding eyes. They hurled questions and accusations at him, and he saw that none of them believed him. He was cold with despair, he knew how thin and wild the story sounded, as only truth can sound, but he was determined to keep his head through the chaos that had descended upon him. Back deep in his mind somewhere was one steady reassurance.

He did not believe Floria had made any mistake. She had merely started to say something and had not been able to finish it. What little she had said had given a false impression. Every abominable bit of circumstantial evidence conspired to make it look like the truth. When she regained consciousness, she would finish what she had started to say, she would clear him with her first words. If she never regained consciousness— Karl shivered at the thought. But he kept his balance

94

through the fear that rode him. An innocent man couldn't be caught in such a trap without some avenue of escape, without some weapon of truth to deliver him. There had to be a way out, if he held to the truth.

Then he wanted to shout in relief at a sudden thought that flashed into his tortured brain. The bullets the men had dug out of the wall! He would demand that they be sent to a ballistic expert. They would be proved not to have come from his gun. He shot a boring glance at Todd.

"Where are the bullets you dug from the wall?"

"Soupy Groggs has got 'em. What does that matter? Why don't you just make a clean breast of it and spill the whole business, you poor fool? We might have a little less contempt for you if you did. Come clean and be done with it."

"I didn't do it, I tell you!" Karl's eyes were half mad. "I didn't do it! I haven't any more to say. I've told all there is to tell. It doesn't make a damned bit of difference to me whether you believe it or not. If you are determined not to believe it, if you don't know me any better than to think I could do a thing like that, nothing I could say would get me anywhere. Didn't anybody go for the sheriff?"

"No." Riceman shook his head. "Frank wouldn't let 'em. He commanded us to keep the whole thing quiet till we got hold of you. He sent the boys out to look for you, they saw you coming with Bert, rode back and said so. We haven't any of us told Frank yet that you're here."

`What did he tell the doctor?" Karl interrupted.

"Not a damned thing," Riceman snapped. "Only that he was to go ahead and do what he could, and keep his mouth shut. The rest of it's up to the sheriff. Well, it's going to be a nasty job for whoever does it, but somebody's got to tell Frank that Karl's here. Bert, maybe you'd better go in—"

"Bert can stay here and mind his own damned business," Karl cut in harshly. "And you too. I'll tell Frank myself."

"You're crazy!' Riceman barked. "Stark, roarin' crazy. He'd kill you the minute you stepped in the room. You're not going. Grab him, Todd!"

"Get out of my way!" Karl faced them with grim features, his eyes ugly and threatening, his heavy-sinewed hands doubling at his sides. "I'm going! Try to stop me and I'll knock you cold, the whole damned bunch of you! Get out of my way!"

Groggs had been watching from the kitchen window. He had seen Karl go into the barn and had remained motionless by the window, waiting for him to come out again. He stepped from the kitchen door, leaped across the porch and came hurrying down the steps to intercept him. Groggs' broad lantern-jawed face, so oddly incongruous with his stout burly body, was working with emotion. He stopped squarely in Karl's path. Karl halted, a breath of relief sucking into his lungs.

"Soupy, where are those two bullets Todd and Lafferty dug out of the wall? I've got to have them."

"Anybody can have 'em, for all the good they'll do 'em," Groggs answered meaningly, his voice hoarse with distress. "If any fella got aholt of your gun to try to frame you, Karl, it's a hell of a lot of good it'll do him. I got them bullets from Todd, and I melted 'em down into a shapeless hunk of lead and threw 'em into the ash can."

Karl set his teeth on a groan. The fates *could* think of something worse. They were drawing the trap tighter at every turn. "But why?" Karl demanded, his voice shaken by fury and despair. "In God's name, what did you do that for?"

Groggs held his eyes, grim, loyal. "Because. Now no ball expert can git hold of 'em and prove that they come from your gun."

Karl gritted his teeth. "Yes, you poor misguided idiot! And neither can he get them and prove that they *didn't* come from my gun! Oh, you poor fool, why did you do that!"

Groggs was a quaking mass of remorse. "I thought—I didn't know—I was just tryin' to help—"

Karl turned from him and raced on toward the house, leaving a shaking and demoralized Groggs staring at his disappearing back. Then Groggs whirled, cried loudly, "Karl!" and came lumbering after him. Karl stopped and wheeled about.

"What?"

"It—you got to—I'm a fool. Of course it wasn't you. He was on Bounce, though, I saw him."

"It wasn't Bounce, Soupy," Karl explained patiently.

"The fellow caught up Ball. You couldn't tell Bounce from Ball that far away unless he was in the bright sunlight."

"It just might have been Ball," Groggs conceded. "But if things looks bad for yuh, ain't there some good lie you could make up to—"

"I'm damned if I'll lie!" Karl snapped. He recounted in six short sentences just what had happened. "The boys don't believe me. You can see how it looks."

"It looks like hell," Groggs agreed. "But the boys is damned fools not to believe yuh, if you say that's what happened."

Karl stared. "You mean to say you believe me?"

"Do I look like a fool?" snapped Groggs. "Didn't I say *if some other fella* had got your gun? Shut up and go on in and see Frank. He's about crazy." He turned away, and Karl hurried on into the house, chaotically blessing Soupy Groggs, who believed.

His head was roaring so badly that he could scarcely get his thoughts together. Groggs had taken his last chance of proof from him. In a mistaken effort to destroy evidence that might, be against Karl, remembering that Karl carried the only thirty-eight in the territory, he had jammed the younger man more tightly in the trap. Karl staggered like a drunken man, more mad than sane, as he went up the steps, stumbled across the porch and into the kitchen. In another moment he would be face to face with his father. Frank could kill him if he would, but he had to see him. He had to see Floria again. It might be for the last time. He staggered through the empty kitchen and shoved open the door to the living room.

No one was there. The door to the room occupied by Frank and Floria was closed. The house was still as a grave. There was no sound anywhere, save the sound of a fly circling around the window, buzzing in the last rays of the sinking sun. Karl halted and tried to straighten his shoulders, and his gaze went absent-mindedly to the fly, and back to the closed door. His shoulders sagged in spite of him, and his feet kept stumbling as he blundered toward that closed door.

Then he reached it, groping for it, and threw it open. There his feet failed, and he stopped, like a man abruptly stricken with paralysis.

Floria lay on the bed, white and motionless, barely breathing. Frank sat on a chair at the foot of the bed, erect, still, waiting, his eyes swathed by a blood-stained bandage, his features like a face carved out of pale brown granite. By the head of the bed, leaning over it, gazing steadily into Floria's face, sat Dr. Plesstree.

Plesstree was an old-timer in the district. His hair was white now, but he was still the most dependable and efficient doctor the John Day territory had ever known. If there was a man who was a stauncher friend of Frank than old Doc Plesstree, Karl could not name him.

At the sound of fumbling steps and the opening of the door, the doctor turned his white head and glanced up. His thin wrinkled face was worn and sagging. He spoke in a subdued undertone. "Good evenin', Karl," and turned back to his patient.

Karl sat in the rocker, rigid and still, his mind straying after erratic and irrelevant things. He thought of the buzzing fly in the next room, battering itself against the window pane, striving to reach the sun's last light. He wondered what the fly was doing now that the sun had gone down and taken the day with it. He noted the clock on Floria's bureau had met with some accident. The glass was cracked across the face. He caught the dull glow of the twilight on Floria's perfume bottle, sitting back of the clock. The bottle was arresting to the sight. Its shape was odd, its stopper was of brightly colored glass, shining black and bright scarlet. Frank was always buying such little trinkets for Floria every time he went to Heppner or Sundown.

Karl's gaze went back to the doctor, at the sound of movement. The thin little man had risen from his chair to light the lamp on the stand beside him. As the light glowed and the flame on the wick steadied, Plesstree replaced the chimney and returned to his chair. The old man's face was very weary, his eyes haggard and drooping. Karl glanced at Frank. The blinded man had been drooping in his chair, fighting off sleep and the exhaustion of shock and pain, but the exhaustion had won. He was sound asleep, slumped sidewise against the arm of the chair. Karl's gaze turned back to Plesstree.

"Doctor, do you think she'll come through all right?"

Plesstree shook his head slowly, regret darkening his tired eyes. "It ain't possible, Karl. She's bleedin' internally, and I ain't got no way of stoppin' it. Nobody could stop it. I ain't had the courage to tell Frank yet. She may last another day. No longer."

"You're worn out," Karl said abruptly.

A wan smile crossed Plesstree's face. "Yes, I am. I've been goin' it for thirty hours without a let-up, and I ain't so young as I used to be. Can't stand the pace like I used to. But I'll see this through all right."

"Go in my room and lie down for a couple of hours," Karl urged, infinitely touched by the old doctor's weary face and drooping eyes. "A little sleep would put you in a damn sight better shape."

Plesstree turned a closely scrutinizing gaze on Floria's white countenance. "Well—" His gaze came back to Karl. "That ain't such a bad idee, Karl. There ain't nothin' I can do but watch, and you can do that as good as I can. It don't really make much difference whether anybody's here or not. She'll just open her eyes and say a few words and die, or die without ever openin' 'em at all. Nobody can do a thing. But of course we have to sorta sit and look on. Human bein's does them things. Only dogs and brutes can crawl away and die in peace."

Karl smiled wryly. "Yes, I've thought of that, several times. Well, you go lie down. If there's the least change, I'll call you."

Plesstree nodded. "I believe I will. I'm about tuckered out. But I couldn't leave Frank alone with her. It's all right so long's you're here. If she wakes up and Frank wants to have her to himself, you needn't call me till it's over if you don't want to. It won't matter. I won't be able to help her none. You sure you can stay awake?"

Karl nodded, his smile somber. "I couldn't close an eye, Doc. You go ahead and rest."

Plesstree rose, stretched his aching muscles, and went softly out of the room.

Karl heard him go quietly across the living room, into the bedroom opposite, heard the door close behind him. A moment later he heard the slight creak of the springs as the weary old doctor lay down. Then there was silence again, the dull silence of suspense, settling over everything. Outside in the cottonwoods a turtle dove sobbed in its feathered throat.

Karl glanced again at the clock. It had passed midnight. For four hours they had been sitting there waiting. It might conceivably be four hours more before anything of change would come to pass. A chilling fear nagged at his brain. What if Floria died without regaining consciousness? He shrank at what that would mean. It couldn't happen. Even the fates couldn't do so horrible a thing to a man. She must open her eyes, and speak, and finish what she had started to say, she must clear him. For Frank's sake above all others', she must. He sat and stared at her. She lay like one already dead, her face white and sunken, the merest rise and fall of her chest being the one evidence that she still lived.

Karl averted his eyes. He was growing cramped in all his muscles from sitting still so long. He removed his shoes, rose to his feet, and began pacing up and down the room noiselessly, flexing his muscles. As he passed the bureau Frank had bought for her, his gaze again was caught by the little trinkets Frank had got in Heppner and Sundown. Heppner was a larger town than Sundown, lying off to the north. Frank did not go there often, but when he did the trip always meant a new trinket for Floria. The scent bottle, jugs and jars in queer shapes. A fat powder box, deep and round, hugged close to the scent bottle, its lid awry.

Next it was a small glass dog, sitting on a comical little "Chinese treasure chest." The chest was perhaps ten inches wide by a foot long, and it locked by a supposedly secret manipulation of a series of interwoven pieces of wood. Karl half grinned at the childishness of the thing. There was, something childish about Floria anyhow.

He reached out to straighten the lid of the powder box. He hated things awry. His fingers lingered over the funny little wooden chest with its silly little lock. What a queer light-headed idea, for her to imagine that anyone couldn't open the thing. He could do it himself, without half trying, merely by studying the interlacing strips of wood.

A man's mind, driven to the limit of endurance by shock and horror, will turn to the most trivial thing for relief. There was an amused smile on Karl's face as he picked up the little glass dog and set it aside, then lifted the chest. He had no intention of looking into it. He had no least interest in her strings of beads and such articles of feminine frippery. He was momentarily piqued by the puzzle of those interlacing strips of wood, he felt the normal human reaction to the challenge of any kind of puzzle, the impulse to solve it merely to prove to himself that he could do it.

He set the chest down on the edge of the bureau, and bent absorbed eyes on the lock system that was supposed to be intricate, glancing now and then at Floria and Frank to be certain that they had not moved and had no need of him. To his surprise, he found the lock more difficult of solution than he had thought it would be. He moved the strips of wood this way and that, but the chest remained securely fastened. As the puzzle proved of greater intricacy, the more he became absorbed in it. For a grateful few moments he forgot the grim circumstance and threatening menace surrounding him, forgot the bitter tragedy closed into that silent room. He was utterly fascinated by the queer little lock.

Then because it was neither more intricate nor deceptive than its creator had intended it to be, he suddenly moved the right piece of wood in the right direction, and the box opened. It did not open as does the ordinary box, the lid swinging up and back on hinges. By the aid of little wooden springs in each of the four corners of the chest, the lid lifted straight into the air for three inches. Then it reared backward at a deep slant, leaving the contents of the chest fully exposed in one swift motion.

Karl started, then stared incredulously at what lay there. Nothing but bills, currency of several denominations. He judged accurately at the first glance that there must be several hundred dollars there in bills. His eyes widened. What was Floria doing with that money secreted away in this little chest? Did Frank know she had it? Reason told him that Frank did not unless Floria had told him. Frank would never tamper with her trinkets and her silly little secret chest. She would have known it was safe from prying eyes when she put it there.

Karl shook his head, deeply puzzled, and started to close the box, then he caught sight of an envelope lying half concealed by the money, in the left end of the box. It looked familiar, and he glanced at it a second time. It was the letter her father had written her in reply to her request to come home so long ago. Floria had written him again when she and Frank had been married, and he had answered to wish her happiness. So far as Karl knew, he had never written again. But why had she laid this letter away?

A nameless suspicion that all was not as it appeared to be flashed over Karl. He studied for a moment, then he deliberately shoved the money aside, removed the envelope from the chest and took the letter from the envlope. It was not the letter she had shown him and Frank, though it bore the same date. With dilating eyes he read it through, with as impersonal a feeling of investigation as has a detective in sifting evidence. The letter was a warm and affectionate letter from a fond and trusting parent, but the whole of its significance to Karl lay on the second page, which read:

"and you know how sort of lost Fee felt ever since your mother died.

"However, don't you go to worrying about me. I get along fine since I went to live with your aunt Jessie. Me and Jessie always did get along fine. I'm glad you give that Fordham fellow the goby. I never did like what I saw of him. I'm glad you're having a good time up there in the mountains with your friends. No, I don't ever remember hearing you speak of the Sands girls, but my memory ain't what it used to be, so that don't count for nothing. You stay there as long as you want to, and as long as you're having a good time.

"Sure I can send you some money. Did I ever refuse to give it to you when you wanted it? That's one thing about me, Florry. I may be a plain old cuss but I always made good money. I'm sending you five hundred dollars, in bills, and if you want more just let me know. Don't mind if I don't write. You know how I always did hate writing letters. Have a good time and come home when you get ready. Aunt Jessie sends her love and says to tell you she's got a room all ready for you.

Always your loving old dad,
George Milne."

Karl stared at the letter with wrathful eyes. The lying, scheming little whelp! She had forged the letter she had shown to him and Frank, knowing they would never know the difference, never having seen Milne's handwriting. Karl set his teeth against his fury. Women like her he had never known, but he saw through her as clearly as he told himself he should have seen through her long ago. In that moment of revelation he despised her as vehemently as he had once thought he had loved her, despised her most for the trick she had played on Frank.

Frank! Only one thing mattered concerning her. To save Frank from ever learning what she had been. She was dying, and the grief of losing her would be grief enough for Frank. Let him keep his belief in her. The money he would quietly dispose of somewhere where it would accomplish something. The letter he would burn. Frank would never have any way of finding her out.

As he turned away from the bureau, after placing the little glass dog back on the chest, a cold and sneering whisper reached him from the bed.

"What are you going to do with that letter and with my money?"

Floria, the queer look of hardness in her blue eyes, anger in the set of her pale mouth, lay staring at him from her pillows.

Karl's feet felt weighted as he walked toward the bed. His hard flinty eyes were on her white face, but there was no mercy in them.

"I am going to save Frank from ever knowing you as you are," he said evenly. "I'm going to burn this letter and dispose of this money so that no one can ever find them there and disclose their meaning to him. And you—you're going to save Frank too. What was it you started to say to him when you fainted, just after the shooting?"

She gave him back his gaze coolly, almost with something of amusement in her face. She knew that the game was played out. She did not care. "I simply started to say that it was you who told Armor where I was. That you must have found him somewhere and found out who he was, and threatened him if he did not get out. It would be like you. He couldn't have found out where I was any other way. But he thought it was you he was shooting when he fired at Frank. He said so. I heard him. He said 'No country ain't big enough for both of us, Karl,' when he saw Frank fall. Then I screamed, and he fired at me."

"You saw Armor?" Karl cut in, tensely, bending closer toward her. "You *know* it was he who shot you and Frank?"

"Why, of course I know!" The amusement grew in her drawn face. "He was on your horse, too, on Ball. Why, haven't they got him yet?"

Karl shook his head, feeling himself suddenly beginning to shake with relief. "No. Listen. What little you did say, when you started to talk to Frank, was hideously misleading. They all think you were accusing me of the shooting. All the evidence points to me. I can't explain now, there isn't time. But you're the only one who can save the situation. Not to save me, but to save Frank. He's nearly crazed with the whole horrible business. I'm going to wake him, and you've got to tell him before it's too late."

"Wait!" Her eyes were coals in her white face. "I'm going to die, I know that. If I do what you want me to do, there's a price on it. Frank—Frank—that's all you're thinking of. You can take time to think a little bit about me. Where is Frank?"

"Down there at the foot of your bed, asleep in his chair. If you can raise your head a little you can see him."

"It's too much effort. I'll take your word for it. I hate him. I hate you. I hate this ranch. Dull, deadly hole. If I'd gone back home like my father wanted me to I wouldn't be dying. If it wasn't for your Frank, and for your fool tongue, blurting out to Armor where I was, I wouldn't be—"

"Hush!" Karl interrupted sternly. "I know how far I'm to blame without your saying it. Armor thought you'd married me, he thought he was wiping out all evidence of what he tried to do before. It's Frank's ghastly misfortune that he looks enough like me to be mistaken for me through the window. You're right. If I'd said nothing to Armor, he'd never have come here, never have known where you were. I'd give my life to undo it, willingly, gladly. That I can't do, but I can shield you, and I'm going to. Is that your price?"

She smiled enigmatically. "That's it. Burn that letter now, before you call Frank, so that I'll die knowing you can never show it to him. Now, do you hear?"

Karl nodded. Without a word, he removed the chimney from the lamp, thrust the letter into the flame and held it there till it caught fire. When it was well ablaze, he replaced the lamp chimney, placed the burning letter on the small pan on the table in which Frank laid his pipes, and turned it till the last fraction of an inch was ash. He even crumbled the ash with his finger. Then still without speaking to her, he walked down the floor beside the bed to Frank's chair and laid a gentle hand on Frank's shoulder.

"Frank" He shook the shoulder slightly. "Frank. Wake up. Floria wants to speak to you."

Frank started and sat erect in his chair, turning his head hesitatingly, putting out a groping hand. He spoke in a voice blurred by heavy sleep. "Yes? What? Did somebody call me?"

"I did, Frank." Karl gripped his hand and drew him to his feet. "Floria wants to speak to you. I'll call the doctor in a minute. He went to lie down."

"Floria?" Frank followed his son's guiding hand, stumbling in his haste and his blindness. "I didn't know you were awake. How are you feeling now?" His hands groped for her as he reached the head of the bed and went down on his knees beside her.

Her hard blue eyes, mocking, deriding, raised to Karl's face, then dropped to her husband's sightless, bandaged head. "Yes, I'm awake, Frank. But not for long. They should have told you. It seems—it seems that I'm going to die."

"Floria, no!" The swift anguish of the cry made Karl wince. Sands bowed his bandaged head, his shoulders shaken in a sob as his stony control gave way for a moment. "You didn't mean that. You can't leave me. I need you now as I've never needed anyone before."

Over his bowed head, Floria's eyes flashed to Karl, and the racked man started at the expression he saw there. It was plain to read, as plain as if it had been chiseled on blue stone: blue stone was not harder than her eyes then. Nothing was in them but wild rebellion and bitter hate. Rebellion that she had to die, unreasoning hate of the man who had brought the disaster to be. A strange little gleam of triumph shot across the hard blue surface of the staring eyes, too subtle and too swiftly gone for Karl to probe.

Suddenly Frank caught himself into stern control, lifted his sightless face and spoke to her. "Floria, tell me what you started to say when it first happened. You didn't mean that Karl did the shooting, I realize that now. What did you mean? What was it you started to say?"

Her eyes leaped to him, then over him again to Karl. In them flamed all her intense hatred. Her hatred for Karl was perhaps most violent. He had given Armor Fordham some intelligence of her whereabouts. Otherwise she would not be now dying. Reason enough to hate, to her kind. But he had found her out for what she was. For that she could never forgive him. She had neither the justice nor the intelligence to realize that it was not Karl who was to blame for the tragedy wrought, but her own treachery. Her own treachery alone was responsible for her being there, for the train of events that had made her answerable to the inexorable law of retribution. She, being incapable of so fine a point of discrimination, knew only the fierce maniacal rage of retaliation.

Karl had burned the letter, trusting her; his last defense, his last proof of her duplicity, was gone. She had him fairly in her weak dying hands, helpless beneath whatever blow of revenge she should strike. Revenge at the man who had dared to find her out and command her to atone so far as was within her power. She laughed, a half-cazy sound of leering defiance.

"Yes!" With a flare of false strength, vitalized by her wicked hate and her sense of triumph, she struggled to sit up. Her voice shook with fury as it rushed to the condemnation. "That is exactly what I meant. Karl did it. Do you think I could mistake his face? I saw him through the open window just before he fired at you. Karl—" She swayed and fell back upon her pillows. Her voice broke, then came again in a last struggling gasp, the hard blue eyes shot a last malignant glance at the man she had perjured herself on the threshold of eternity to punish. *"Karl did it."*

Dr. Plesstree had heard the sound of her voice. It had brought him awake, its tone, raised and sharp, had called him out of his sleep, though he had not been able to distinguish her words. He came hurrying into the room, but stopped short by the bed at what he saw. One glance at her face was enough. He paused by Karl's side, distressed eyes on Frank's bowed shoulders. Frank's hand groped along the pillow, found her face, and stopped. Touch told him what his eyes could not see. He had heard the doctor enter the room, and he straightened himself, turning up a ravaged face.

"Doctor, are you there?"

"Yes, Frank."

"She is—dead?"

"Quite dead, Frank. There wasn't anything a body could do. I knew it from the first, but I didn't see no use makin' anything harder for you."

"Yes. I understand. Leave me, both of you. I want to be alone with her." The ravaged face was like brown granite again beneath the blood-stained bandage, granite that had faded to a paler ghastlier hue in the heat of a storm. "Karl, remain in the sitting room. Don't go out of the house. Doctor, you know what I told you. Keep what you know to yourself, as much as you can."

"The processes of the law ain't my affair," said Plesstree rather curtly. "All I've got to do is report a death. I shall report the truth. Your wife died of a bullet wound that caused internal bleeding." He turned on his heel and strode out of the room.

Karl followed him. In the kitchen Plesstree picked up the bag he had placed on the table there some time before, and reached for his hat and coat. He turned steady eyes on Karl, standing, a dark bulk in the doorway against the light from the sitting room lamp, his face barely touched by the light of the candle on the kitchen table.

"Karl, have you anything to say to me?"

Karl shook his head, giving the doctor back his look. "No. Only, it wasn't I."

Plesstree grunted soundlessly, nodded, opened the door and stepped out in to the raw chill of early morning. In another moment he was gone, and Karl was left alone with his despair and his appalling thoughts.

He paced the floor, his head reeling with frantic groping. There was only one possible chance for him, to find Barker Christy and force the man to tell the truth. And there was no telling where Christy had got to by this time. He would go as far as he could, that was certain, to put himself beyond the retribution of the law.

Karl halted, tense, in angry rebellion. He should not be held here, helpless, while Christy was free to go as far as his horse could take him. He, Karl, was the only living person who knew, who had the proof, that Christy was the man who had hurled devastation upon the Lazy S. Floria herself had given him the last needed proof. In what he said at the window, the man she knew as Armor Fordham had spoken the proof that he was the Barker Christy who had talked with Karl in Wildcat Canyon a short while before. What he had said had been an insolent retort to what Karl had said to him there in the canyon. And Barker Christy was the only man who could swear to the truth of the facts.

Karl contemplated for a moment the advisability of trying to escape from the house immediately, before Frank came out of the death room, to begin his pursuit of Christy. But second thought told him there would be no least chance of his getting away. The Lazy S punchers were alert and watching. If they saw him trying to get away they would take the act as proof of his guilt and shoot him down without compunction. He could not get to his horse. Leaving on foot would only be more futile.

Into Karl's chaotic thought there intruded a sound, the stumbling thud of Frank's faltering footsteps. Karl halted again in his pacing, in the center of the room, swinging to face the door, listening. But Frank was not coming toward him. He had gone through the other door opening out of the bedroom, into the front room. Karl frowned, wondering what he could be doing in there, what he could possibly be trying to find. Involuntarily, he thought that there was no lamp lighted in that room for a man to see his way about, then with a shock he remembered that Frank would never need a light again.

Rage shook Karl where he stood listening. This was the worst thing that Barker Christy had done. He had killed Floria, but that was a mercy. Sometime she surely would have revealed to Frank what she was, and that would have been worse than losing her by death. Christy had a life to answer for. But he had taken the light from Frank Sands forever, and had thereby committed the worst crime of his reckless days. Karl straightened, hearing Frank's footsteps coming back through the bedroom, toward the door which opened into the living room. In the next moment the blinded man appeared in the doorway, his left hand groping along the wall to close the door as he passed from the bedroom, his right hand held behind him.

He stood still for an instant in a listening attitude, then he spoke. "Karl?"

"Yes. I'm here."

"Karl!" There was a new agony on Sands' face, but a desperate hope fought with it. "Karl, even in the face of everything, I'm wondering if it is possible that she could have made a mistake. Can Bert swear that you were with him from the moment you left the ranch till you returned?"

Karl's face was drawn and dry, like a dirty paper mask, but his head was high, and his voice was steady, almost gentle. "I'm sorry, Frank. He can't. I wasn't with him all the way. If you'll listen, I'll tell you the absolute truth. I've told the boys. None of them believes me. But this is exactly what happened. When Bert and I got on to the ridge we saw smoke coming out of Wildcat Canyon—"

In swift succinct sentences he reported exactly what had taken place.

"I know how it looks," he finished. "I know it sounds thin, wild, even silly. And the only man who can bear me out is Barker Christy himself, alias Armor Fordham. I'll find him and make him do it if I die trying."

Frank's brown-granite face turned gray. "Why should he catch up Ball when he had a perfectly good horse of his own?"

"I should think you'd see that, Frank," Karl returned patiently. "To make an alibi for himself, of course. He had his pinto, the red and white one. I saw it down the canyon a little way when I was talking to him. The killer came here on Ball. If Christy was questioned, he could say he'd been riding his own horse, and show the horse to prove it. Nobody could mistake that pinto for Ball. But the boys could mistake Ball for Bounce. You know very well that they can't be told apart at a little distance."

Frank's face twisted under the bloody bandage across his eyes. "And *you* fired two shots at a coyote—" His voice shook. "Just across Sago Lily Flat—and missed both times? *You?*" Color rushed into his colorless face. Sudden blind rage shook him. "I've always told you that wild temper of yours would do for you some day. I know what drove you. I didn't know till I heard some of the boys talking. You wanted Floria yourself. You couldn't bear to see me have her. You went mad, Karl. Mad! But that doesn't excuse you. Your defense is ridiculous. Thin as water. Utterly unbelievable. I might have known she couldn't mistake your face. Might have known—"

"Frank!" Karl took one step toward him, shaken to

the depths by wild rebellion. "You've got to listen. You're the one that's mad! But you've got to listen. You can't condemn me like this. You've got to hear the truth whether you want to or not. You—"

"You're a damned poor liar," Frank interrupted, suddenly cold in his rage. "She saw you at the window. All your halting attempts to prove an alibi can't nullify her statement and the evidence that upholds it. You're guilty—guilty as hell, and you'll have to pay the price." His face was convulsed by grief and fury. "Why didn't you do a better job of it? Why didn't you kill me too, and spare me this? Why stand there and lie to me?"

Karl had passed the power of control. He cried out hotly. "I'm not the one who lied! She is! *She* lied, I tell you! While you were asleep in your chair I got to fooling with that silly little chest of hers and it came open. In it was a letter from her father that proved her to be a low lying cheat, not good enough for you to walk on. She saw me have it. She was furious. She said if I'd burn it she would tell you the truth. She admitted to me that it was Bark at the window, the man she'd known as Fordham. She heard him say as you fell, 'No, the country ain't big enough for both of us, Karl.' He thought it was me he was shooting— what he said was a direct answer to what I'd said to him in the canyon. She knew she was condemning me, but she hated me. She hated you. Hating both of us, she lied to—"

"*Stop!*" Frank's voice filled the room with righteous

thunder. "You've gone too far! Lying about the dead! Good God, I never knew a man could be so low! You've spoken your own death sentence. The law won't get you. I'll kill you with my own hands!"

He swung from behind him his right hand, and gripped in it was the long ugly-bladed hunting knife that habitually hung on the wall in the front room. He started toward Karl with groping, but steady, steps, his face ravaged by his fury and indignation.

Karl, transfixed by consternation, remained motionless, staring at him dumbly, while terror chilled his skin and crept up the roots of his scalp. He would have little chance against the elder man, and he was only too well aware of it. Sands was imbued with the abnormal strength of rage, and Karl was weakened by the surge of horror and despair.

Karl stood like a stone, his blood pounding painfully in his ears. Frank advanced slowly toward him. Karl bit his lip and clenched his hands. His mind, dulled, frantic, groped back to the dim days of his childhood. Staring into his father's nearing, fury-distorted face, he was on the verge of making a vain wild leap to one side, when he felt his shoulder gripped from behind. Someone drew him silently backward. A soundless whisper breathed in his ear.

"Get out! Quick!"

And Bert Gray stepped solidly on the floor, passing Karl, raising his voice levelly. "Stop where you are, Frank. It's Bert. What's the matter?"

In the same instant Karl, with a wild gasp of relief,

reached the kitchen door in three long steps and flashed out of the room. Sands halted, non-plussed, dashing the knife out of sight behind him.

"Karl!" he shouted.

As Karl went out the kitchen door he heard Bert answer. "Karl just went out. I passed him on the way in. I wanted to ask you—"

Frank's voice broke in a terrible baffled cry. It was the last thing Karl heard from that room as he dashed out into the early morning, and stopped short, confronted by Groggs.

Without a word, Groggs grasped his arm and hurried him toward the barn, where Bounce was standing, saddled and waiting. Groggs motioned Karl over the fence, and Karl fairly threw himself into the saddle. Groggs followed him, stepped close, and gripped the reins. His worried eyes bored into Karl's. His broad lantern-jawed face was scored by a grimace of distress. In the first chill of the daylight, he faced the man in whom he alone had faith.

"Bert and me was afraid of what might happen if the missus died, so we been watching. We saddled Bounce, and went up there to the house to listen to what was goin' on. We wasn't gonna interfere unless we had to. There's been mess enough around here already. Don't you blame Frank, kid. He's too het up to know what he's doin'. Once he cools down and kinda gits over it, he'll come to his senses. These other fools around here give me a pain in the neck. But they ain't knowed you, like I have. You hang on, and don't git rattled. You'll come out of this all right. Now, you go to town and give yourself up, see?"

Karl frowned. "Give myself up?"

"Yeah." Soupy Groggs nodded, and winked broadly. "Unless you can give 'em the slip. That's the understanding I got cooked up for you, to get you out of here. You go into town and give yourself up. Todd and Lafferty is goin' to follow you, and you don't dare try no gittin' away while they're on the job. They'll shoot you outa the saddle and think they're doin' their fool duty. You'll have to go straight to the sheriff's office, all right. But I reckon you can use your head after that. They ain't goin' in. They're just gonna see that you go there, then they're comin' back. That's the best I could do."

Karl smiled grimly. "It's enough, Soupy. Keep a stiff upper lip, old-timer. And take care of Frank. I'll see you later, somewhere."

Groggs grunted his unintelligible monosyllable and blinked. "You git out of here. That's all you got to do. And—use that head of yourn."

Karl smiled, pulled himself up in the saddle, and turned Bounce toward the road that ran along the river back to join the road to town. As he passed the barn, Todd and Lafferty rode from behind it and fell in to the rear. Karl's face set in the semblance of a hewn mask. He rode on.

He had a long trip ahead of him, and he settled himself to the ride automatically. He was worn physically and mentally, half stupefied by the whirl of events during the last several hours. The sharp morning air braced him for a while, and he looked up with grateful eyes to see the morning light growing above the rim rock breaks. He knew from the light in the sky that the hour must be nearing four o'clock. He should be able to reach Sundown by noon.

He wanted to make the best time possible. He wanted the business over with. He was so completely weary that his brain went dead on him for a space. He had a sudden feeling of everything going blank. He was almost as unconscious as a man asleep. Only his senses of scent and hearing were vaguely alive. He heard the birds in the trees greeting the morning. He heard the faint hullabaloo of a coyote chorus back in the mountains. He heard his horse's hoofs striking rhythmically in the dust and on the rocky ledges. He smelled the pungent sweetness of the sage, the tang of the pines. How long that queer state of hearing and smelling only continued, he never knew.

He came to himself abruptly, confused and bewildered, it seems hours later, astonished for a moment to find himself astride Bounce, on his way to Sundown. He shook his head, striving to clear his brain of its daze. Why was he there? What had happened? Behind him he heard a familiar sound, the sound of Lafferty's high-pitched short laugh, and remembrance came back to him in a flood. He was on his way to give himself up to the sheriff, and Todd and Lafferty were trailing him to shoot him out of the saddle if he made any attempt to escape.

They had known him for years, yet they could believe this atrocity of him simply because a weird train of dovetailing circumstantial evidence made him look to be the guilty person. If Karl Sands had suddenly gone bad, what of it? You never knew what anybody was going to do.

Karl blinked his eyes, like a man whose sight is suddenly blurred. The world was against him. Every hand and every face—but Soupy Groggs. To Soupy, the king could do no wrong, no matter how things might look. A little smile barely touched Karl's lips. His brain automatically turned from that phase of thought and began methodically seeking some way out.

The sheriff, of course, would give him a fair trial by law. What would that gain him? Karl's slight smile grew grim. Gain him? The rope. He was level headed enough to see that such evidence as weighed against him was hopeless damnation. All that he could say in defense of himself would sound like the wild thin story Frank and the men had condemned as such. With no one to pursue him and bring him to account, Barker Christy would ride out of the country never to be seen again, and Karl Sands would be damned by false evidence, by the testimony of the men and his father, and by a woman's lie.

Then, without any least connection in his mind to bring the thought, he abruptly thought of Jeudi Payne. He thought of her as one suddenly, standing knee deep in blood and mire, might perversely think of a pearl pink lily growing by a pool in the forest, unsullied and fragrant, a far scene of something fair cutting like a breath of mountain air into the miasma of a cesspool. Jeudi. And he knew something that he had never known before. He knew that he loved her. Two paramount things may bring a man to that sudden realization: the one of seeing a face again after a long absence, the other of unexpectedly bidding farewell to a known face never to see it again. Neither thing brought knowledge to Karl. He had not seen Jeudi for months. He had not said good-by to her never to see her again. The thought simply came.

Like a ray of revealing light breaking into the darkness, it came and showed him what he had not known before. He loved Jeudi Payne. He had always loved her. But there had been no sudden sweep of emotion, no blinding passion that all but carried him off his feet. There was only the settled possession of something that had always been unique and irreplaceable in his scheme of things. He had thought he loved Floria. He knew more surely than ever now exactly what he had felt for her. He shuddered at the thought of what she had been. And he had been such an idiot that he had not realized till now that he loved Jeudinow, when it was too late.

He was sunk in absorbed thought, as Bounce traveled steadily and ever nearer to Sundown. He was seeing Parkin's Place in his mind's eye. Parkin had but three other girls in the house. He had rooms upstairs over the saloon and dance hall and the girls lived there. Karl bit his lip in vexation. He did not know which room belonged to Jeudi. He would have to learn that after he got there.

It was slightly past noon when he came to the great red bluff that reared above Sundown. As he approached it, he saw the little town lying in its narrow valley on the river's edge, distant and unbelievably beautiful, like a little toy town on the bank of a toy river, a thousand feet below him. Then the trail swerved, and the view was shut from his sight. Bounce turned into the twisting trail that began to descend the face of the bright red rock bluff.

A S HE RODE down the one main street of Sundown, Todd and Lafferty drew nearer, came within a few yards of him and held that close surveillance. He came to the little frame building where the small but imposing sign of SHERIFF OF GRANT COUNTY hung in the window. He halted Bounce, then he suddenly turned the horse about and rode up to face Todd and Lafferty. They both drew their mounts to a halt, eyeing him warily, suspiciously. Karl looked them steadily in the face, first Todd, then Lafferty.

"I just want to tell you that I hold nothing against you," he said quietly. "If this thing ever comes straight and you know the truth, I bear no grudge. Perhaps if I were in your place I'd be making the same mistake that you are making. It may not mean anything to you, but I wanted to say it—now."

Todd looked at him uneasily, distress in his face, and shifted in his saddle. But Lafferty sneered openly. His hand dropped to the butt of his revolver, and he addressed Todd with sharp warning.

"Watch out! He's trying to pull some trick and give us the slip."

Karl smiled and shook his head. "I'm not, Laff. I just wanted you to know that, that's all. You might be glad to remember it some day. I'm going in now and give myself up to Whiteside." He wheeled his horse and rode back to the sheriff's office.

As he swung from the saddle to the ground, he saw that Todd and Lafferty were right behind him. They halted directly in front of the door, watching him closely, dour and hostile. Without even glancing at them again, he walked into the office.

Sheriff Whiteside was sitting in a chair, his feet upon his old battered desk, half asleep. He was a short broad man, with great shoulders, an imposing girth and a great head. His bushy hair thrust out around his heavy face like a mane. His brows were wide and bushy, drab brown like his hair. His rough-hewn face was smooth shaven. He rubbed his eyes and straightened in his chair as Karl entered and paused before him. He saw Todd and Lafferty halted before the door. He grinned lazily at Karl.

" 'Lo, Karl. What're you doin' in town?"

"I came to give myself up," Karl said clearly, loudly

enough that he knew his words would carry to Todd and Lafferty. "Get up and lock me in a cell."

Whiteside stared. His sleepy brown eyes opened, and grew as blank as the side of a wall. He seemed to freeze in his chair. His mouth fell open. "Huh?" he blurted. "Did you say that? Or am I dreamin'?"

"You heard me correctly," Karl returned, his face rather set. "Will you get up out of that chair and lock me up, or do I have to do it myself?"

Whiteside drew a long deep breath, exhaled it slowly and took his feet off his desk, carefully, and set them down quite as carefully, as if he were afraid of making a noise. He stared through the door at Todd and Lafferty. Karl turned and looked at them. They sat stiff in their saddles, outlined against the clear hot sunshine, gazing into his face with intent eyes. For the first time there was the beginning of a doubt of their own convictions in their faces. Lafferty silently took off his hat.

"Come on, Todd," he said gruffly, and the two wheeled their horses and rode away.

Karl turned back to the sheriff.

Whiteside still sat in his chair, his hands now on his knees, motionless, his unblinking gaze on Karl. "What the hell have *you* done?" he demanded.

In his ears, clear and loud, Karl heard Frank's voice—"tell the truth." He answered without hesitation: "I haven't done anything, but they think I have. I'm to tell you exactly what has happened." He did it. "Take it or leave it," he finished. "That's the truth, with nothing left out. Frank believes her. You can't blame him. The boys believe her and the evidence. You can't blame them. What do you believe?"

Whiteside stared helplessly. "I ain't believin' nothin'. So far as you're concerned, it looks like hell. The boys are right, so's Frank. That's about the wildest story I ever heard. About the wildest story anybody ever told, and the thinnest. I've seen you shoot too damn much to think you could miss like that. But any man *can* miss. Barker Christy left this neck of the woods months ago and he ain't been heard of since. But—he coulda come back. If you're tellin' the truth, there'll be Bark to catch. I'll lock you up and send out a posse to round him up."

"You won't." Karl held his gaze with hard eyes. "I'm not armed. Bert or Todd or somebody took my gun. I don't remember which now. But you will not lock me up. Send a posse out after Bark, thrashing around everywhere and raising hell, and you'll never catch him. I'm going out on a still hunt after him, and I'm going to bring him in, if I die trying. I'm going to walk out that back door of yours into the alley, and you can shoot me in the back if you want to. But you won't. Down in your heart you know I'm telling the truth, crazy as it sounds. You're going to let me have a chance to prove it. After I'm gone, give me an hour—then raise all the hell you want to."

Whiteside scowled. "Are you plumb crazy?"

"Not quite. It's a wonder I'm not, at that," Karl smiled dryly. "You raise hell, and accuse me of the murder, and set the whole town looking for me. That'll keep their minds off Bark. If word gets to Bark by any chance, he'll think he's clean, and that I'm caught tight. He'll show himself—maybe join in the hunt for me, and I'll get him. Are you too flabbergasted to know logic when you see it?"

Whiteside shook his head. "It's almost too damn' logical." His eyes narrowed. "You better forget it. I'll have to lock you up, I guess." He rose and deliberately drew the gun swinging from his wide belt. "Start out that door, and I'll have to wing you."

Karl's gaze did not waver. "You won't. I'm going. Although, I'm warning you now, if I never find Bark I'll never come back. I refuse to hang for something I didn't do. Keep your shirt on, Whitey—I'm gone."

He turned and walked deliberately toward the back door of the room. He did not look back. Whiteside slowly raised his gun, his thumb cinched on the hammer and slowly pulled it to full cock. The bore of the weapon pointed accurately at Karl's back. "Come back here!" he commanded hoarsely.

Karl had reached the rear door. Without turning, he opened it and stepped through it. He closed it softly behind him. Whiteside stared first at the door, then at the cocked gun in his hand. His heavy rough-hewn face was quite without color. His hard forefinger compressed the trigger of his Colt slightly, his big thumb gently lowered the hammer. He sank into the chair from which he had risen. Once again he drew a great breath, and exhaled it slowly, as if it hurt his lungs.

The door through which Karl had gone gave onto a short narrow hall, on each side of which was one small iron-barred cell built of two-by-four timbers. From the farther end of the hall another door opened onto the alley. The door stood open. Karl passed swiftly down the short hall, through the door, and into the alley behind the building.

Straight down the alley, four buildings beyond, was the back entrance to Parkin's Place. In less than sixty seconds Karl had turned into that door and was hurrying cautiously up the stairs. None of the girls was to be seen. He tapped guardedly at the door of each of the four rooms, but got no answer. As he turned, baffled and apprehensive, from the last one, he saw the slatternly little drudge girl who cleaned up about the girls' quarters and kept things generally in order for Dutch Parkin. One of the four rooms was hers. She was coming up the stairs with a pail of soapy water in one hand and a stained old ragged mop in the other.

She gazed at Karl with dumb cow's eyes. She had seen him about the place down stairs a few times, but he was no more to her than simply some man that came to Parkin's Place. She did not know who he was, but she did know that Parkin made it a strict rule that no man was allowed on that floor. If any man wanted Floss or Mame or Tess to himself there were booths downstairs for that kind of thing. If Dutch ever found a man up there he was liable to kill somebody. She couldn't remember that any man had ever had the temerity to come up there before, and she was frightened. She walked hurriedly up to Karl, staring at him with scared eyes.

"What you doin' here?" she asked, in a whisper.

"Where's Judy?" Karl countered, swiftly.

"She's downstairs eatin' breakfast with the other girls. If you wanta see her you better go down inta the saloon. Dutch don't allow nobody up here. He finds you're here and he'll half kill yuh."

"I have to see Judy, and I have to see her here," Karl told her sharply. He drew a half dollar from his pocket and slipped it into the hand that held the ragged old mop. "You go down and tell her, and keep your mouth shut. You won't get into trouble. Only, hurry! Go down and tell Judy I'm waiting up here for her, but don't let anybody hear you tell her."

The girl gazed avidly at the edge of the coin, sticking up between her thumb and forefinger. Then she raised her gaze to Karl's face. "I don't know yuh. Who'll I tell her?"

"Tell her it's John Blade," Karl answered impatiently. "She'll know who it is. Get out, quick!"

The girl shook her head, still frightened, and partly undecided. But she went. She set down her pail and mop and went silently down the stairs in her worn old shoes, gripping the coin tightly, and turning once to throw a dubious glance back at Karl.

He shrank into a corner of the hall, into the shadow which was thick there. He dared risk nothing. He half crouched there, holding his breath in suspense, waiting. It was less than five minutes before Jeudi came into sight, hurriedly ascending the stairs. To Karl it had seemed an hour. She descried the bulk of his tall figure in the corner, and stopped a few feet from him, trying to penetrate the shadows with her sharp gaze and distinguish his face.

"I don't know any John Blade," she said curtly, her voice low and angry. "What the devil do you mean by coming up here like this? If Dutch knew it he'd—"

"There isn't any John Blade," said Karl swiftly. "That was merely some way to get you up here."

Jeudi caught her breath, and her face flamed so brightly that he could see the light upon it there in the dingy hall. A look of incredulity swept into her wide black eyes, and she stepped close, putting out a hand toward him.

"Karl! You! *You* came to see *me?*"

"Where's your room?" Karl demanded. "Take me in, quickly. I've got to talk to you."

She went still for a bare instant, sensing urgency of unspeakable import in his voice. Then she whirled, caught his arm in a tight grip, and hurried him to the last door on the left side of the hall. She shoved open the door, thrust him into the room ahead of her, followed him and closed the door. She stood there, clearly revealed in the bright sunlight streaming through the wide window, leaning her back against the closed door, her eyes scrutinizing him intently. The vivid color faded slowly from her face, leaving it the color of smoked ivory.

"What's wrong?" she whispered. "Why did you come to me like this? What's happened?"

He stepped closer to her and looked down into her eyes. "So much has happened that it will take a few minutes to tell you. It's too ugly for your ears, but you have to know." In rapid brief sentences, he told her. He told her the whole of the grisly story from beginning to end, while she stood listening with widening, shocked eyes. When he had finished she drew a deep painful breath, as Whiteside had done, and let it escape from her lungs in little gasps.

"My God, Karl! What a horrible mess. And those poor fools don't believe you!"

Karl looked suddenly like an old and weary man. His rugged blond face was bitten deep with lines that were to leave a mark forever. The mask of suffering engraved there was creased by a thin smile. "Soupy Groggs believed."

A bright smile flashed across her dark face in answer. "Yes." Then her smile was gone, leaving a somber little countenance. "But you mustn't blame Frank too harshly. He is broken and bewildered."

"I don't blame anybody. Why should I? They can't help believing what they think their eyes and their brains tell them. *They* didn't see Bark there in Wildcat Canyon with his new thirty-eight Colt. *They* didn't see that damning letter Floria had hidden in that fool box. They did what they thought was just, and I'm doing what I *know* is just.

"That's the difference. That's that. I'm going to get

away somehow, and make for the mountains back up the river."

"You don't think Bark left the country?" Jeudi put in quickly.

Karl answered with a negative shake of the head. "When he knows damned well how easily a man could hide forever back there in those pine thickets? Not on your life, Judy. He'll stick right there, till he sees that things have blown over, and then he'll ride quietly out of the country and keep going. That's why I've got to move now, and move fast—before he considers it a safe thing to make a move. When the town goes cock-eyed with excitement over my escape and begins hunting for me, he may be sly enough to show himself and join in the hunt."

"I doubt it. " Jeudi frowned. "No, you're right in the first place. He'll stay in hiding till you're held for it, or till it blows over. But how are you going to get out of here?"

"I don't know." Karl stepped close to her, and laid a hand on either of her shoulders. She paled swiftly, but she did not shrink from the touch. "I've something else to say before I make the dash," he said softly. "I love you, Judy. Did you know that?"

"Yes." There was an ancient wisdom in the black eyes. "When a woman loves a man, she always knows. But I never thought you'd tell me. I thought Frank had talked to you against me. I saw the way he looked at us the last time you were here. I never thought I'd see you again."

"He did try to keep me from you," Karl admitted. "But—I thought I was in love with Floria. Funny, isn't it? I thought I was ruined for life when she married Frank. Men are unreasonable brutes, Judy. It took Floria to make me realize at last that I loved you."

"Thank God for poor despicable Floria," said Jeudi.

Karl looked at her curiously. "Queer. You're not excited. I'm not, either. What makes us so cool and collected? How can you be that way when you've suddenly admitted that you love somebody you'd die for?"

"Cool?" She laughed, softly. She stepped close, slipped her arms around his neck and laid her head on his breast. "You only think you are. Kiss me and you'll know better."

Something rushed through Karl's veins, dizzying him. His arms dropped around her, and he gripped her tightly to him, lowering his face to hers with a rush. He felt his blood pounding in his ears.

"Judy!" His voice was shaken, breathing through her hair like a breeze. "Judy." The shaken tone dropped to a whisper. "My Judy."

"Yes, dear. Always. Now and for ever. Nobody else's. But listen, Karl. We have to think of your safety, first. You have to get away."

He straightened, looking down into her face, still gripping her tightly, his blue eyes ablaze. "I know it. But I can't think for just a minute yet." He suddenly laughed aloud. "Judy, Judy! What do you think of a man who's been in love with a girl for years and didn't know it till somebody whacked him on the head?"

She smiled. "It's been done before."

"Well, that doesn't excuse me for being a blockhead. We know it now, and I guess we'll have to be satisfied with that. But my God, woman, think of the time we've wasted! We could have been married a couple of years ago."

"Married!" Jeudi went very still in his arms. Her black eyes clung to his face in amazement. "You're sure you mean that?"

Karl sobered. "Well, for God's sake, what did you think I meant? Judy! You aren't that dumb, are you?"

"Not when you talk that way. But I know how people can think, Karl. And you say that Frank did try to keep you away from me. I know what arguments he used, too. That it wasn't for you—Jeudi, of the dance hall. But when you talk like that, Karl—I know what I have to do. I've been thinking of it for days, weeks. You never did know anything about my mother, did you, Karl?"

"Don't tell me unless you want to, Judy." His arms held her closer.

"I suspect I have to tell you." She smiled up into his face, and her slender right hand sunk itself in the thick blond hair that waved over his head. "She was a dance hall girl, too, Karl. She worked years ago for Dutch Parkin. He was in love with her. So was everybody else, I guess. She didn't care anything for him. That was a long time ago, when Dutch had a place in The Dalles. He followed her about like a dog, and was about as faithful as one. She fell in love with a fellow who came there to The Dalles on business for his father. He fell in love with her, too, but his people were pretty straight-laced. They raised Cain with him when they found out he was coming there to see her."

"He—listened to them?" Karl interrupted her.

"Not then—but later." Jeudi's black eyes were deep. "He was engaged to another girl, and you can see how it looked to them, Karl. Their son, brought up in the way he should go, engaged to a girl of good parentage, who loved him, falling in love with a dance hall girl. Oh, they made it pretty hot for him. There's no doubt of that. But he was mad about mother. He deliberately took her across into the state of Washington and married her, brought her back to Dutch's place and told Dutch. Dutch was dubious about it, I guess it nearly floored him, but he wanted mother to have anything that could make her happy. They all decided to keep it quiet for a while, until he could break it gently to his people.

"He went back home and broke it off with the girl he was engaged to. He said he didn't love her and he couldn't marry her. He wouldn't give any other reason. His people were nearly mad about it, and the girl was heart broken. She was angry, too, and she wanted to show him she didn't care. Right in the face of it, she up and married another man, right when his people were bringing every pressure they could to make him and her make up. He went and told mother all about it.

"His mother was prostrated by the disgrace of the

whole thing, as she called it. She took to her bed and the doctors said she was like to die. He told mother he'd better not see her till things quieted down a little, then he'd claim her before all of them and take her home, and they could go to hell if they didn't like it. But when he went home mother talked it over with Dutch. She knew she was going to have a child, but she hadn't told my father. She told Dutch. She talked it all over with Dutch, and anything she wanted to do was all right with him."

"And then," said Karl slowly, "was when she made a mistake?"

Jeudi nodded. "Yes. She said she didn't want to ruin his life. She knew what the people would think and say if he ever took her to his home, the way they'd treat her. She knew he'd never come back till his mother was better—and his mother knew it, too. She might be sick long enough for him to get over it. Mother told Dutch that it was so hopeless, she wanted to go away where they'd never hear of her again. Her name was Madge Deveau. Dutch says she was beautiful. He'd have done anything for her. Just to please her, he sold his place and went away, a long way away. Then I was born. My mother met my father on Thursday. They were married on Thursday, and I was born on Thursday. So she named me Jeudi, which is French for Thursday."

"Didn't she ever see your father again?" Karl broke in, impatient to hear the end.

"Never again. She died before I was a year old. He

138

never knew what became of her. When I was only eight years old, Dutch came to Sundown. We've been here ever since. When I was twenty years old, Dutch gave me a letter to read, a letter my mother had left for me to read on my twentieth birthday. That's how I know all that happened. It's all been in my mind for the last few weeks stronger and stronger, when time kept passing by and you didn't come any more. I'd never have said or done anything if you hadn't said you loved me—that you wanted to marry me. But now I know that I have to do what I've dreamed of doing for a long time."

Karl held her back a little way and looked intently into her eyes. There was a queer breathless tone in her voice. He felt her body trembling. "Judy! What do you mean? What are you going to do?"

"When you go away to from here to hunt Bark Christy, I go, too." The breathless tone grew. Her voice broke into little gasps of excitement. "You go—to hunt Bark Christy. I go—to the Lazy S."

Karl started in astonishment. *"To the ranch?"* He thought of Frank Sands' warning concerning Jeudi Payne. "Judy! Why, in God's name do you want to go there?"

"Because, dear—" Jeudi's eyes shone. "Frank Sands is my father."

Karl started again, and cried out, holding her back till he could see her face, staring down at her incredulously. "Judy! Are you—are you sure? Frank—your *father?*"

Jeudi smiled steadily. "Dutch has always known it. That's why he brought me here. Frank never even knew he had a child. When Dutch had his place in The Dalles he was awfully slim, and he wore a heavy beard. He didn't go by the name of Dutch Parkin. After mother died, he began to get heavy, and before he came here he shaved off his beard, he thought he was so changed Frank wouldn't know him after all the years, especially if he changed his name. And Frank didn't. Mother told me who my father was in that letter she wrote before she died, when I wasn't a year old."

"I begin to see a lot of things." Karl's voice and eyes were slightly dazed, unable to comprehend the entire significance of what Jeudi had said, at least till he had given the astounding revelation a moment's thought, swift thought, intensive and searching. "I see why my own father hated Frank."

"Dutch says he hated him till the day he died," Jeudi replied, her black eyes staring back through long years lying under the dust of the dead. "And Frank's mother wasn't pretending, either. She really died from her shock over the mess she thought he made of things. You were born only a few months after I was, and your mother thought so much about Frank that you look like a second edition of him. That made your father hate him worse. Yet, when he died, he wanted Frank to have you, because your mother had loved him. And Frank loved my mother, and he always loved her. He never married anybody else, because he couldn't forget her."

"But didn't he ever know what became of her?"

Jeudi nodded. A little wave of sadness swept over her, for the pain and the tears those others had known so long ago, she felt their quiet ghosts in the room, listening to her, nodding in agreement to her slow words, perhaps wiping away a furtive ghostly tear. She nodded again, and her eyes were wet.

"Yes. Dutch sent him a letter, telling him she had died, and he signed it with his own name, the name under which Frank had known him. It doesn't matter what that name is. Dutch'll never use it again. He's Dutch Parkin for ever."

"I suppose it's the best way," Karl agreed. "There would be no use—"

He cut himself short as there came the sound of heavy footsteps hurrying up the stairs.

"Dutch!" Jeudi whispered. "Be still. I've locked the door."

They both turned noiselessly to face the door, as Parkin's heavy steps clumped down the hall, and halted there. His heavy fist banged on the panel, and his voice rose to assail their listening ears, harsh with anger.

"Judy!"

"Yes, Dutch." Jeudi's answer was steady and clear. "What do you want?"

"I want to know who you got in there!" Parkin snapped. "You answer me quick! Who's in there?"

Jeudi braced herself, straightening her slender shoulders. "Dutch Parkin, have I ever lied to you?"

"No," he retorted, biting off the word. "And don't start now, yet. Who's in there?"

"Dutch!" Jeudi advanced till she was close to the door, and her voice sank to a steady, vibrating tone. "Dutch—if there was a chance for me to have everything in this world that I ever prayed for, if there was a chance for me to go to the kind of life you've always wanted me to have, would you take it away from me?" She listened a moment. He made no answer. "Or—would you help me to get it?"

There was a long silence on the other side of the door, then Parkin answered with curt impatience. "Don't ask me such silly questions, yet. Who you got in there?"

Jeudi answered swiftly. "Come in and find out, Dutch. He's in trouble, and he came to tell me about it. He's in trouble, and he's got to get away quietly. I'm going to open the door, and I want you to come in here and add your wits to ours. If anybody can think up some quick way out, you can." She heard Karl's almost soundless gasp, and whirled to speak one swift sentence. "It's the only way, Karl—if you trust Dutch he'll die for you."

She stepped to the door, unlocked it, and threw it wide. Parkin stood there, huge and glowering, and his little green eyes leaped to Karl's face. He came ponderously into the room. His gaze held on Karl's face. He did not even glance at Jeudi. She closed the door behind him and locked it again.

"So it's you?" Parkin said to Karl. "I thought it was.

Suky said Judy was up here with some man. I slapped her mouth and told her I break her neck if she says that to anybody else. Hmmm. Nigger in the woodpile, ain't it?"

"What do you mean?" Karl countered quietly.

"Well, what you think? Bass Todd and Clink Lafferty, they come down from the Lazy S. Into my house down stairs they come, looking for you. They leave you at the sheriff's office, they get a drink at my bar, they go back to see if you're there, and Sheriff Whiteside he says you get away already. Todd and Lafferty they come back lookin' for you, yet. Sundown she's gone crazy. Everybody out lookin for you. They say you got mad and killed the missus and shot Frank up. They tell plenty all right. It don't sound good for you, neither. Then I think it kind of funny you get away so quick. Suky comes down and says some man's up here with Judy, and I got a pretty good idea who it is, too. So I come up to find out."

"You never told anybody—" Jeudi cried out, but Parkin cut her short.

"*Mein Gott,* Judy. Do I shoot off my face, what?" He scowled at her in heavy reproof, then he swung his belligerent gaze on Karl. "Well, what you got to say? What you doing up here with Judy where I don't allow nobody?"

"What did Todd and Laff tell you I said?" Karl eyed him warily, ready for anything.

"They say you told 'em some cock and bull story, but they don't say what it is, yet." Parkin's gaze wan-

143

dered from Karl to Jeudi and back to Karl again. "What you got to say? I'm waitin'."

Jeudi cut into the conversation peremptorily, stepping close to Parkin and laying a hand on his arm. "Dutch, this isn't the time for any washy sentiment. But you've got to know how things lie. I loved Karl from the first time I ever saw him, like my mother loved Frank Sands. He's asked me to marry him. He—"

Parkin interrupted, a slightly startled expression flashing into his little green eyes. "In that letter, she told you about Frank Sands, no?"

"She told me everything, Dutch." Jeudi's voice was abruptly gentle. "All about you. Things aren't going to happen to Karl and me like they happened to mother and Frank Sands. If I was only Jeudi, the dance hall girl, he'd never let Karl marry me—but when he knows I'm his daughter, it will be a different story. See, Dutch. After all the years, you've been so faithful, and it's going to come right."

"Maybe," said Dutch heavily. He suddenly sat down in the nearest chair. "So—you going to leave me, yet. She—I liked her, too. And—you going to leave me."

Jeudi's eyes were wet. "I have to, Dutch. My father needs me. He's blind. He's broken. He needs somebody that means something to him. He needs me. I've got to go to him."

"Yes." Dutch nodded. "You got to go, I guess. But you—" He turned weary eyes on Karl, and his great body seemed oddly helpless, as if it had received some mortal blow. "What you been up to?"

Again Jeudi interposed. "Tell him everything, Karl. Don't leave anything out."

Karl hesitated only for a fraction of a moment. Then he launched into bald swift speech. Again he related the grim happenings on the Lazy S. Parkin sat listening, never once taking his eyes off Karl's face, till the last word had been said, the last harsh fact told. Then he shook his great head, slowly, his gaze fastened almost unseeing on Karl.

"Well, I got no way of knowing if you're tellin' the truth or not. But it makes no neverminds. If Judy believes you, I guess you ain't lyin'. Anyway, I've knowed things to happen that sounded crazier than that. And I never yet kicked no dog when he was down. All that got nothing to do with it, though. If Judy likes you, and you been all right with her like she says, I do what I can."

Jeudi's hard-tried control broke. Like a little girl, she threw herself into Dutch's huge arms, buried her face against his monstrous breast and broke into wild sobs. "Oh, Dutch, Dutch!"

"Here! Here!" Dutch's green eyes blinked rapidly. "Cut that out! What you want me to do, eh?"

"Dutch!" Jeudi sat up on his knees, and her white face flamed with eagerness. "If you could only get him away, somehow! It's not going to be easy, with the town all worked up and on the lookout for him. But if you could only get him away."

Parkin's stare grew helpless. Things were moving too fast for him. He shook his head from side to side

145

like a bewildered mammoth, and his green eyes fastened on Karl.

"So you can go get Bark Christy, huh? Where you want to go?"

"Back into the mountains north of the ranch," Karl answered instantly. "He's hiding up there in the thickets somewhere. Somehow—I don't know how, now,—but somehow I'll find him, if I can just get there."

"Your horse, Bounce," said Dutch. "He's in my stable yet. Whiteside he brought him in and left him, told me to unsaddle him and put him up. I look him over good. He's got your gun stuck in the side pocket yet. I took it out. I got it put away."

Karl's smile flashed into quick light across his haggard face. "Soupy's put it there! I didn't know it."

"*Ja.*" Dutch sighed. "Somebody put it there, all right, and a handful of shells, too. Well." He sat erect, one arm around Jeudi, and looked quizzically into her face. "If I got to get him out, I guess I got to do it. Wait, let me figure." He sat staring at her, his green eyes almost closed, his slow-moving brain worrying ponderously at the problem that had been thrust upon him. Then he began to smile, a sly shrewd smile, and he turned to look Karl up and down with calculating gaze. "Let's see, how big you ain't. Hmm. Big enough, yet! I bet you I got it, though. Jerry, he goes by Heppner tomorrow with the big wagon, to get me some supplies down there. He got to have a lot of feed sacks and kegs in the wagon. It's a long trip to Hepp-

146

ner. It takes Jerry three, four days to go there and back. He got to sell a horse for me, too. Fella I know up that way wants to buy Jingo."

"You don't buy supplies in Heppner," Karl protested, a faint suspicion creeping into his eyes. "You buy in Prairie City. The railroad comes to Prairie City."

"*Ja*," Dutch agreed. "The railroad comes to Heppner, too, no?"

Karl stared at him, steadily, trying to puzzle out Dutch's intent. Heppner lay almost due north, a long trip by the road, over the hills and across the canyons. Prairie City lay almost as far away southeast by east, deep in the mountains. Dutch had traded in Prairie City for as many years as Karl could remember. He could not remember when Dutch had ever sent Jerry to Heppner for anything What was the man planning? Karl gave up.

"You're one ahead of me, Dutch."

"*Ja?*" Parkin shrugged and scowled. "Well, you want to get into the hills up north of your ranch, ain't it? Then Jerry goes by Heppner tomorrow to get me some supplies. Nobody pays any attention to what I do. Jerry got lots of sacks and kegs in the wagon. I guess nobody going to look under those sacks and among those kegs when Jerry's he's driving my wagon yet, even if he goes to hell for stuff. Jerry don't talk much. Only when he has to. Even then he don t say nothing. Do I got to knock you down to make you see something, *ja?*"

"Dutch!" Jeudi sat up rigidly on his knees.

"Oh, shut up, Judy!" Parkin scowled fiercely. There was something dog-like in its devotion deep in his green eyes. "You always get what you want, don't you? If it's to go to your father, I guess you go. If it's Karl, I guess you get him. And you—" The huge man's eyes glared into Karl's. "You get that Christy fella and show him up what he is. But if you're lyin', and just tryin' to get away yet, I come after you and choke you with my own two hands. Py Gott, *ja!* I do that!"

Karl smiled, a thin grim smile that was little more than a grimace. "I'll get him. And I'll never forget this, Dutch! I never had any idea what there was inside of you till Judy told me what you'd done for her and her mother. And when I come back, Frank's going to know, too. I never forget anything people do for me and mine, Dutch. And Judy's mine."

Dutch Parkin smiled. Both Karl and Jeudi were looking into his face, and at sight of that smile they wanted to weep. They knew he was seeing over their heads, Madge Deveau. He lifted Jeudi bodily, got to his feet and gently placed her in the chair where he had been sitting. He took a ponderous step up to Karl, and laid a heavy hand on the younger man's shoulder. For a moment he remained silent, erect, and something about him filled the silent little room with a passing breath of majesty. It was his memory of Madge Deveau. Then he spoke, and his booming voice was little more than a rustle, like a ghostly breeze moving through green bay leaves, leaves that were fragrant and could never die.

"You be good to Judy. For her. That's plenty for me. All right. You come along with me, now. I give you dinner and take you where nobody sees you, so you can sleep. You look all done up, yet. Judy, you can sit here and make dreams for a while yet." He turned and walked heavily toward the locked door.

Karl turned to the slim dark girl, and she rose to meet his advance. He took her in his arms, held her close for one brief moment, and laid his lips gently on her forehead. "Till—then!" he whispered, and followed Dutch out of the room, leaving her to sit and make her dreams.

The great Dutchman led him by a devious back route to a room in the cellar where he kept numerous kegs and boxes. There he brought Karl a substantial dinner and a big pot full of coffee. Karl made himself a makeshift couch on some boxes with some sacks, ate to repletion, stretched out on his hard bed and dropped into the sleep of exhaustion, while the town seethed with excitement, looking for him, and while Dutch Parkin's place went on with the business of life unmindful of his presence. He slept, while Todd and Lafferty and the sheriff combed Sundown from end to end and could not find him. He slept, while day waned into night, and Todd and Lafferty rode back to the ranch chagrined, to tell Frank Sands that Karl had escaped and left no trace behind. He slept straight through till morning.

Down the alley, across from Parkin's Place, was a

large livery barn. Parkin owned and ran both livery barn and dance hall, so that it was a simple matter for him to hitch one of his teams to the big wagon and drive it up the alley without anyone being the wiser or giving his actions a second thought. It was not yet dawn when he awakened Karl, and guided him into the alley where the wagon waited, half filled with kegs, boxes and sacks. Jerry was waiting, dozing, on the driver's seat. With no difficulty, Karl was utterly concealed in the bed of the wagon, leaving no suspicious bulk under the carelessly spread tarpaulin to attract the attention of passersby.

Karl reached out from under the sacks to grip Parkin's hand.

"I'll tell you what I told Judy, Dutch. Till—then."

Parkin gripped the hand, shot him a penetrating glance, and blew out his lantern. He grunted meaninglessly and turned away.

Jerry chirped to the horses, the wagon jolted, and rolled down the alley to the street. He drove leisurely, because that was his habit. The vehicle was well out of town long before day broke. Jerry was shriveled and old, thin and dour, with an imp's face and a satyr's eye. He carried a gun that looked big enough to topple him over, and if he had one quality more pronounced than his disinclination to talk it was loyalty to Dutch Parkin. Not once during the whole morning did he speak to Karl.

As the hours advanced toward noon, Karl felt and heard the jolting halt of the wagon. Then it started on again, and by the increase in the jolting he knew that Jerry had driven off the road. They traveled on for a little way farther, then the wagon stopped again. For the first time that day he heard Jerry's voice.

"Better git out and eat."

Karl crawled out of the wagon bed, out from between the kegs, out from under the sacks and the tarpaulin. Jerry had driven into a sheltered spot beside a creek, well out of all sight of the road. As Karl dropped lightly to the ground, and straightened to his height to stretch his cramped muscles, he glanced at the wagon. He smiled. Dutch Parkin, when he made a bluff, made a good one. Hitched to the wagon were two black horses. Tied behind the wagon was a third black horse, Jingo. Only a very discerning eye could have told the three horses apart, but Frank Sands had sold Jingo to Dutch, Karl had broken the horse. He turned his smiling gaze from Jingo to Jerry.

Jerry was hurricdly spreading on a sack some cold beans and bread, some tin pans for the food, and a couple of spoons.

"Better eat. No coffee. Dutch said not to build no fire. You eat while I feed the horses. Be with yuh in a minute."

Karl grinned. "All right, Jerry. Guess I'll wash some of the dust off my face first." He went down to the creek and splashed the cold water over his face, laving away the dust from the kegs and meal sacks. He wiped his wet skin on his bandanna handkerchief and came back to the meal just as Jerry finished feeding the three horses. The men ate hurriedly, in utter silence. When they had quite finished, Jerry looked at Karl and spoke again.

"Better git back in the wagon."

Karl grinned again, and obeyed. The wagon rumbled back onto the road, and continued its journey. Part of the time Karl slept, fitfully, wondering just what orders Dutch had given Jerry. It was late afternoon before he learned. The wagon turned from the main road and proceeded across the rolling surface of a long slope, beneath the branches of the red-holed pines, across the thick carpet of hot pungent needles, where wagons usually did not go. A good mile away from the road, the wagon stopped again.

"Well, we're thar," Jerry announced mildly.

Karl crawled out of the wagon again. Jerry looked at him with a comical little twinkle in his impish eyes. He pointed to the horse tied to the back of the wagon.

"Know that critter, eh?"

Karl nodded an affirmative reply. "Of course. Jingo. Dutch said he was selling him."

Jerry turned on the wagon seat and surveyed the black horse, a horse that was very black indeed, with no white markings on him anywhere. The comical twinkle in his eyes grew.

"Yeah," he drawled. "Does look like Jingo all right. But if he had four white socks and a white star on his forehead, who'd he look like? And if Bounce suddenly was to git all black, who'd *he* look like?"

Karl started, and a slow smile crept up to his eyes as

he caught Jerry's meaning. "How could Bounce get all black, Jerry? And how could Jingo get four white socks and a star?"

Jerry shrugged. "Oh, Dutch, he's slick. Little black and white paint, that's all. I bet you anybody that happened to go into Dutch's stable and see that horse all suckered up like that'd swear he was Bounce, too. Your saddle's under the seat. Here's your gun." From under his capacious coat, the surprising gnome of a man drew Karl's thirty-eight and extended it toward him, butt first. "And here's the ca'tidges." He dug a handful of cartridges from his pocket and gave them to Karl.

Karl paused, on his way to untie the horse whose disguise had deceived even him. He turned surprised eyes on Jerry. "What you going to Heppner for, Jerry?"

Jerry gaped at him, astonished. "Why, supplies. When Dutch says git supplies in Heppner, I git 'em. Hurry up."

Karl shook himself into action, stepped up to the head of the horse and reached to untie the rope. Bounce nickered and nosed his pocket. Karl chuckled, and stepped back with the loose rope in his hand. Jerry laconically tossed his saddle and bridle to the ground a few feet from him. The saddle blanket followed. Karl glanced down at Bounce's paint-blackened stockings, then up at Jerry, as the little man chirped to his team and started to turn his wagon around.

"One on me, Jerry!" Karl called. "Much obliged."

"Thank Dutch Parkin," Jerry snapped. "It ain't none of *my* funeral." And the wagon rumbled on. Within a few seconds it had passed out of sight beneath the trees, to return to the road and resume the journey to Heppner.

Karl picked up his saddle and saddle blanket, and threw them across Bounce's back. He talked to the horse as he saddled him, as men do talk to horses they have ridden and valued for a long time.

5

BACK IN SUNDOWN, Jeudi stood in her room and looked about the familiar walls. They would never know her again. To only one of the house would she say good-by, to Dutch. She had gathered up all her belongings and packed them into an old trunk Dutch had given her. She was ready to go, yet she was like some who come to strange cross roads: she knew the one she was to take, yet she paused for a moment, gazing down the stretch of the other two roads her feet were never to tread, and she wondered just where they led and what was at the end of them. She was oppressed by that sense of loss that is inevitable, when one parts from old familiar ways and scenes.

She had put on her best dress, a plain straight-lined little gown of dark red, unadorned save for a turn-over ivory-white collar. She put on her yellow straw hat with the red poppies across the front, and stood and looked at herself in the flecked mirror that hung on the wall. She surveyed her face minutely, and a half smile lit her black eyes. What would Sands say? She shrank a little and turned quickly away from her reflection. Better not think about that. She walked swiftly to the door and let herself quietly out of the room without a backward look.

Downstairs in the small back room where the girls habitually cooked and ate their meals, Parkin was waiting for her, with a fire in the old stove, a pot of coffee on one lid, and two fried eggs and two slices of bread. As she entered the room, Jeudi stopped and looked sharply from the huge man to the table. He had just set the things out for her, as neatly as he knew how, and he sat waiting beyond the narrow table, his face turned, his mouth pursed under the jutting yellow mustache, his green eyes gazing through the window into the breaking dawn.

Jeudi suddenly wanted to cry. Dutch Parkin had never been known to try to get breakfast for anybody before, at least not as far back as Jeudi could remember. He turned his big head quickly, as he heard her footsteps lightly on the floor. His gaze looked at her, through her, and beyond her. She knew what he was seeing. He was seeing her mother, and the days that had been twenty years ago.

"Is Karl gone?" asked Jeudi.

Parkin nodded, unsmiling. "*Ja.* He been gone a couple of hours, yet. You sit down and eat while your breakfast is hot. I pour you some coffee."

She advanced to the table and slipped into the chair

he had ready for her. She had been endowed with the blessing of tact. She did not thank him for the unprecedented favor of preparing her breakfast. She laid aside her hat and broke a slice of bread, while he lumbered to his feet and brought the steaming coffee pot from the stove.

"You like your coffee nice and hot, no?" Parkin asked anxiously.

Jeudi nodded gravely. "Yes, that's just right, Dutch." She never drank coffee, but she did not look up into his expressionless face.

"You take sugar in it, yet?"

"Just one spoonful, Dutch."

He measured it out carefully. Once his great hand shook, and it spilled a little. "Is that enough, *ja?*"

"Well, just a bit more." Jeudi eyed the spoon as if the amount of sugar put into the coffee were a matter of tremendous import. "There, that's fine. And a little cream, please." She might be able to swallow it with better grace if there were enough canned cream poured into the cup.

"Is there anything else you want, Judy?"

She shook her head. Somehow she managed to smile, and she found the power to keep back the tears that were smarting her lids. She need not have feared his detection of her perturbation: his eyes were blinded by old dreams. Dreams that could never come true. His brain was capable of only one thought: Jeudi was going away, forever. He returned slowly to his chair, and sat very erect in it. Looking upon the scene with an impartial eye, one might have been persuaded that here was Caliban striving clumsily but humbly to serve an archangel.

Jeudi picked up her knife and fork and cut across an egg. "Won't you have one of these eggs, Dutch? They look awfully good."

Parkin looked down at the eggs, at the bright orange of the yolk welling from the cut Jeudi had made. "I ain't hungry, he answered. "I don't eat very much in the morning." He ate enough to feed a horse, four times a day.

"The eggs are just the way I like them," Jeudi assured him. They almost choked her. Rather, the lump in her throat, that swelled every time she looked at him, almost choked her, each time she tried to swallow. But she ate both slices of bread, she ate the eggs to the last morsel, and she drank the coffee to the last drop.

"You want anything more?" Parkin asked, as she set down the empty cup. He had the poignantly gratified air of a Caliban who had served his archangel well and had been blessed for his faithfulness. "You want something else?"

Jeudi turned her face and looked full into the anxious little green eyes that clung to her features—like eyes looking their last upon the dead. "No, Dutch, dear." She had never called him dear. "I'm full, clear up. It was a lovely meal." Dutch never knew that he had forgotten to bring butter. "Is there—is there anything you wanted to say to me?" She almost broke, there. But she had the strength that slender little women often have. She blinked very rapidly and her black eyes shone like lacquered jet. "Is there any advice you wanted to give me before I—before I start?" She could not say before I go. Before I go—it sounded so final.

Parkin tried to sit straighter. A judicious frown crossed his heavy face. He raised one big hand to smooth back his mustache, and she saw that his palm was wet with sweat. A smile lifted his mouth, a set smile, that looked as if he had forced it into place with determined fingers.

"Well, no." He cleared his throat, and swallowed. "I guess you don't need no advice. You—you look awful pretty, Judy. It's too bad he can't see you, yet. Ain't it?"

Jeudi's smile was shaky. She got abruptly to her feet and reached for her hat. "He knows how I look, Dutch. Well, my trunk's all ready. You better call Rusty to bring it down and hitch up the team."

"Rusty's busy." Parkin got to his feet with unusual lightness of movement. "He's goin' to tend bar till I get back. I get your trunk right away." He strode out of the room without looking at her, and she heard his heavy tread going up the back stairs. He never trusted the Place to other hands, so he never drove anywhere on a trip of any length. He was driving her to the Lazy S Block.

She stood beside the table where he had left her, and she found suddenly that she was crying, silently, stinging tears that would no longer be kept back. He was so dumb in his pain, so pathetically eager that she should see no regret for her going, she felt his grief filling the room like the penetrating, bittersweet odor of burning sugar. Her eyes ached with it. Her throat ached. She heard him coming back down the stairs, and she dashed the tears from her eyes. She put on the wide hat, pulling it well down till it shaded all her face.

He was walking down the hall with her trunk on his shoulders, and he called back to her in a voice he tried desperately to make casual. "Gott, what a country. The sun's only just up and it's hot already, yet. We better git started pretty quick. You come on, Jeudi. I had the buckboard hitched up nearly an hour ago."

She followed him out into the street that lay quiet and deserted in the early light of the first sun's rays. The buckboard stood before the hitching rack, where the two gray horses were tied. Dappled grays of clean build and satin skin. Parkin's prided horses. She saw why the buckboard had been got out an hour ago. Every fleck of dust had been laboriously washed from it. Dutch had taken the best blanket off his shelf in the saddle room and spread it over the hard seat. He carried her trunk to the buckboard and placed it carefully in the back of the vehicle. Then he turned to her gravely as she approached.

"Wait, I help you in yet. You might git your dress dirty." He lifted her bodily and deposited her in the buckboard.

She took her place on the seat. Hc untied the horses, got into the buckboard and sat beside her. He slapped the lines on the horses' backs. They started briskly down the street toward the wooden bridge that crossed the John Day.

He said nothing till they had reached the brow of the bluff, and the little town of Sundown lay far below them, a third of it revealed in the morning sun, two-thirds of it still asleep under the shadow of the bluff. There Parkin looked back.

"Kind of pretty, ain't it?"

"Like nothing else on earth," Jeudi agreed.

Another five miles. Then: "You know, Jeudi, I bet you Karl got some idea where that Christy went to. *Ja?* When you got one man after another one like that, you got to go by which is the smartest. That Christy he ain't no fool, exactly, but he got somebody to git away from when he tries to git away from Karl. I bet you—" He had found the one grateful topic that made it easy to loosen his tongue.

From there onward to the Lazy S, he kept up a running fire of talk concerning Barker Christy and Karl Sands. Twice during the journey he stopped by a twisting creek to serve Jeudi with some of the luncheon he had packed in a box under the seat. He would eat nothing at the first stop, but at the second one, when he was certain she had had all she wanted, he finished all there was left. During all the rest of the time he talked about Karl as constantly as if he were afraid to pause lest the flow of talk once started could not be renewed if it ever were stopped. He said the same thing over at least a hundred times, but neither he nor Jeudi noted that.

When the sun was dropping out of view behind the tops of the pines and they came within sight of the ranch buildings on the fiat beside the river, he went silent again as suddenly as he had become garrulous. They crossed the wooden bridge, and drove down the road toward the house. Within a few yards of the ranch house, Parkin halted the buckboard and looked about with critical eyes, at the house itself, at the big log barn, the corrals, the bunkhouse, the feeding flat, the tall cottonwoods lining the river bank, at the horses and the milch cows in the corral beside the barn, at the pigs in the pen. Nothing escaped his scrutinizing gaze. He nodded, satisfied with what he saw.

"*Ja*. It's a good place. I never seen it before."

He got out of the wagon rather stiffly, lifted Jeudi's trunk down and carried it to a spot a little way from the front of the house, and left it there. He returned to lift Jeudi from the seat and place her on her feet on the ground, with much solemnity. Without looking at her, he got back into the buckboard and picked up the lines. Just once he cleared his throat. Just once he swallowed. Just once he spoke.

"Well, I got to go, yet. Good-by, Madge." He never knew that he had said it. He turned the vehicle about smartly and sent the horses down the road at a brisk trot.

Jeudi watched him with hurting eyes till he was shut

off from her sight by the trees along the river. Then she whirled and started blindly for the house. She had never seen the Lazy S, either. She did not see it now. She saw nothing but Dutch Parkin's heavy ugly face, muscle-cramped with the grief that was utterly inarticulate. She walked unsteadily, because her sight was blurred by that image.

Jeudi went slowly up the front porch steps, stood a moment hesitatingly before the closed front door, then realized with a queer feeling of bewilderment that this was home to which she had come. She opened the door and stepped into the front room onto which it gave. She paused, listening, but she heard no sound. She advanced quietly across the room to the farther wall where two doors stood closed, within a few feet of each other. She opened the door to the right. It opened into a bedroom, where a still sheeted form lay rigid on the bed. With a little gasp, she hastily closed that door and turned to the other.

She opened it, to see beyond the living room. She stopped short. Frank Sands sat in a chair beside the window, slumped in an attitude of complete dejection. His arms lay flaccid along the arms of the chair. His bandaged face was set in the dark image of a wooden idol, etched deep with lines of bitterness.

He had heard the sound of her steps, the opening of the door. He raised his head, quickly, turning his face toward her. The expression of his stony features did not change.

"Is it you, Groggs?" he asked quietly.

"No." Jeudi crossed the room to stand before him. "No. It's Jeudi."

Sands almost leaped out of his chair, so violently did he start. The mask of his face broke and grew alive with utter bewilderment.

"*Judy!* Judy Payne? But—what are you doing here?" He got to his feet, a hand outstretched toward her. "But, sit down. Sit down, and rest. It's a long trip. How did you come?"

Jeudi sat down in a chair facing him, swept with relief. Perhaps it was going to be easier than she had thought. "Please, you sit down, too. I'm in the rocker, right before you. Dutch brought me, in the buckboard."

"Dutch brought you!" Sands echoed, his amazement growing. "Why doesn't he come in?" He sensed something of great import in her presence, and a kind of wariness just touched his face. "Isn't he coming in?"

"No. He had to go right back," Jeudi explained, suddenly frightened. If he was so amazed merely at her presence, what would he do and say when he heard what she had to tell him? Her tongue suddenly stumbled over difficult words. "I—I heard what had—what had happened, to you. So—I came."

The bewilderment in Sands' face smoothed, as he thought he understood the reason for her coming. "Oh, I see. Why, Judy. You came all the way out to the ranch to—to tell me you were sorry? You're kind, Judy. I'm grateful." He smiled, the hard grief and bitterness quite erased from his features by the surprise of her advent, by the warmth of gratitude that welled in him at her thoughtfulness. "You're just in time to have supper with me. I haven't been able to eat much. I can do better, with a bit of company."

"I'll stay longer than for supper—if you'll let me." Jeudi twisted her hands together in her lap. "I'll stay all the time, if you'll have me. I brought my trunk. It's out in the yard."

Sands went rigid in his chair, his face turned directly toward her, as if his sightless eyes were straining to see through the bandages and the eternal dark. He echoed her words, not certain that he could have heard correctly. "Did you say you came to *stay?*" He was silent, and the air in the still room pulsed with his bewildered thoughts.

"I'm afraid I don't understand, Judy. Why should you come here, to stay? Did Dutch—see here, there isn't some trick in this, is there, Judy?"

"No—there isn't any—any trick of any kind." Jeudi felt her lips tremble. How was she ever going to find the right words? "I just thought you really need someone, don't you? You need someone to do things about the house. Just to do things, you know, and kind of look after you."

"Judy. Wait." Sands raised a silencing hand. "Give me time to get an understanding of this. Do you really mean to say that you came here to remain, to keep house for me, and help me—because I can't see any more? Karl isn't here, Judy."

164

"I know." Words came easily, because he had said that. "I know that. I came because of you. I came *only* because of you. Couldn't you think of letting me stay?"

Sands shook his head, slowly, astonishment as yet the only emotion of which he was feeling strongly. He was profoundly touched. "Let you stay?" His voice was hushed, wondering. "I don't believe I could make you understand how much I appreciate that. I can't remember when anyone has ever wasted that much consideration on me before. What ever made you think of such a thing, Judy? Did Dutch advise you to do it?"

Jeudi shook her head, without thinking, then suddenly realized that he could not see the gesture of negation. "No. I really thought about it myself. Dutch didn't know I had any idea of coming till I told him. I just wanted to come—so I came."

Light suddenly swept upon Sands. For an instant his face grew terrible in its grief and wrath. "Judy! You've seen Karl!"

"Yes. But later—we will talk about Karl. First—there is something else. If—if you can bear to hear it."

Like steam blown upon cold glass, an almost visible film passed across Sands' sightless face, blotting all emotion from it, all expression. His voice turned cold, wary. "Yes? Well, you may feel free to tell it, Judy. After the last two days, I can bear to hear anything. What is it?"

Jeudi became abruptly aware that she was trembling. She removed her hat and laid it on the table within arms' reach of her in the middle of the room. The light headgear had suddenly become too heavy to be bearable. She pushed back her thick black hair with a shaking hand. Sands stirred impatiently.

"Well? Why don't you speak, Judy? What is it that you have to tell me?"

Her reluctant tongue spilled five hurried words. "Do you—remember Madge Deveau?"

He started as though she had stabbed him. His bandaged face turned pasty white, so slowly that she could see the blood ebb from his skin. He stiffened in his chair and his hands gripped the arms of it till his knuckles showed.

"Madge Deveau?" His voice was harsh. "By what right do you speak to me of Madge Deveau?"

Jeudi did not answer. Some sharp instinct impelled her to silence. Slowly the color crept back into his face, but his rigid pose did not relax. Like Dutch, he had gone back into the land of long memories, where she could not follow, to the burial ground of old dreams that had never come true. Abruptly his rigid pose broke, he relaxed in his chair, his tensed fists spread slightly, and the color rushed back into his whitened knuckles. He drew a breath that went to the bottom of his lungs. He spoke gently, as if something delicate and shy had entered the room, and he did not wish to frighten it away.

"I don't know why you should ask me that, Judy. Yes—I remember. I have *lived* to remember. But what is it to you? What was she to you?"

"She—" Jeudi's voice shook, and her hands clenched in her lap till they hurt each other. "She was my mother."

"You—your mother!" Sands counted a century in the next breath. That something shy and delicate that had entered the room grew warm and living, brushed lightly against his hair: he felt its touch, he heard its whisper in his ears—"Ah, but didn't you *know* I would leave you something behind so that the dreams shouldn't quite die?" Sands swayed in his chair, then stretched out a hand to Jeudi, as unerringly as if he could see her clearly. His long fingers closed jealously around her arm. His voice rose, triumphant, queerly as if he were answering some question she could not hear.

"But of course I know! I've always known! Only, I didn't know what it was I knew. And Dutch Parkin is Merry Devers. I'd ought to have known that, too." His voice broke in an unintelligible cry, and he reached out both arms, gathering Jeudi to him. His sightless face went down on her shoulder. "I ought to have known!" He chided himself, his words muffled against the dark red dress. "I ought to have *known.* Jeudi means Thursday."

Jeudi wept then, because her black eyes could stay dry no longer. They were like two children hugging each other and crying after they had been lost from each other for a long time and had suddenly found each other again.

Soupy Groggs came in from the kitchen, and saw

them there in each other's arms. He stood for a moment staring in incredulity, his lantern jaw slack, his eyes blank. He turned and started out again, but Sands had heard his feet crossing the kitchen floor. The rancher released his daughter from his arms, and got quickly to his feet.

"Groggs! Is that you? Come here, this instant. I've something to tell you."

"Yes, sir, it's me." Groggs drew hesitatingly closer to him, eyeing both Sands and Judy in amazement. "'Tain't nobody else."

"Groggs!" Sands swept out his arm, in that strange unerring sense of direction, gesturing toward Jeudi. Do you know who this is?"

"Sure," Groggs answered, glancing at Jeudi askance. "It's Judy Payne, from Parkin's Place."

"Wrong, Groggs!" Sands laughed aloud. "It's Judy Sands, from the land of Never-Never. My daughter, Groggs. Her mother and I were parted by a—it doesn't matter. She died. We were parted shortly after we were married, not because we wanted to be. I didn't know till today that I had a daughter. Do you hear, Groggs? Go out and tell the boys. Tell Sundown. Tell the whole world. My daughter has come home."

Groggs stared at Sands as if he thought the rancher unexpectedly bereft of his senses. But he knew. He looked sharply at Jeudi, and found her black eyes intent and anxious upon him. He smiled, a kind of sheepish and ingratiating quirk of his wide mouth. He hadn't to look back through too many years to see the meaning. Frank and that Madge Deveau had been married, and nobody had known anything about it. Then it penetrated to the cook's slow brain what such a revelation could mean to Frank Sands. He glanced furtively at the closed door behind which the dead woman lay, the woman who was to be buried in the morning. His gaze grew luminous as it swung back to Frank's face. Let him forget.

With outstretched hand and beaming face, Soupy Groggs advanced on Sands and Jeudi. "Well, ain't that great! I never had no idea! I never knowed you and Miss Madge was ever married, boss. And there was Miss Judy right in Sundown all this time and nobody knowed nothin' about it! You reckon I better tell the boys right now, boss? They'll come tearin' in here like a pack of locoed coyotes. Maybe I better wait a while before I tell 'em?"

"What is there to wait for?" Sands laughed again. Laughter was in him like sudden light, or new spring coming down over the breaks, or old dreams reborn. "Get out of here, you old pelican! You're a barefaced fraud! You're dying to tell them. Get out!"

"Yeah, boss. Yes, sir. Yessir." He went out rubbing his hands together, chuckling to himself.

Jeudi smiled, rather shakily, but there was another thought clamoring for utterance than the excitement of Soupy Groggs. "Father—did you hear what he said? He remembered my mother!"

"Oh, yes, of course he would." Frank's smile grew a little wistful. "He was working for my father when

Madge and I were married. Judy! What—what was that you just called me?"

Jeudi started, her face sobering. "Why, I—what should I call you?"

"Just that. I only wanted to hear you say it again."

He bit his lip, and turned away his face. "Judy—dear—" He turned his head, listening. A smile broke over his features. "Here come the boys."

The Lazy S cowboys came rushing in through the kitchen in a state of subdued hilarity, hilarity over the unbelievable news Groggs had brought them, subdued because they remembered the dead woman whom both Sands and Jeudi had forgot. They gathered around father and daughter in a press, all of them trying to shake her hand at once. She was not Jeudi of Parkin's Place. She was the boss's daughter. They were all rather incoherent, but they managed to make themselves understood. They expressed their delight and approval of the ways of Providence in as many ways as they were individuals. Then they trouped out again, leaving father and daughter to each other. Groggs hurried to the cook shack to get up such a meal as he had not cooked in years.

For a while after the men had gone out, there was silence. Then Sands turned to his daughter, sat down again opposite her, and leaned forward, one hand reached out to touch her. "Judy—you saw Karl. What did he tell you?"

Jeudi drew a breath of relief. "I was afraid you wouldn't let me talk about him."

Sands smiled. "That would be the expected thing to do, I suppose. I don't believe I could want to forget Karl, no matter what he did." His face grew tired in a breath, color faded from it, lines bit into it, he seemed old and sad, and grim. "I want to know what he said to you, and where he has gone."

"He told me all there was to tell. He told me the truth you refused to believe. He has gone to find Bark Christy."

Sands' mouth drooped into a line of settled resignation. He had suddenly remembered the dead woman in the next room. "I can't blame you for believing anything Karl would tell you, Judy. It's always easy to believe those we love. But Floria saw him, at the window. Saw him clearly, heard some sound that attracted her attention and looked squarely into his face, just as he fired. You didn't know her, Judy, or you'd understand. I mean you would understand why I know she could have made no mistake, and could not have lied."

"She did—" Jeudi bit back the words on her tongue. The woman was dead, in the next room. Sometime Frank would have to believe that she had lied. But the girl could not say the words, not with Floria lying dead only a few feet away.

Sands shook his head. "When he can bring Barker Christy here and prove to me by what the man says that his wild yarn was true, I'll believe him. Not before. But don't you see what that would make her, Judy? A woman who would lie to me, dying, to poison

171

my mind against my son and to make my son out a murderer? Good God, Judy! Nobody could believe that of her. No, he's guilty. There isn't anything else to believe. He's guilty."

"He's not!" Jeudi flamed passionately. "He's gone to find Christy and bring him here and make you believe! He's right here in these mountains, hunting Barker Christy!"

Jeudi erred only slightly. Karl was eleven miles from the Lazy S. He was following down Wildcat Canyon, trying to find some trace of the way Barker Christy had gone. That day on which he had burned the brush with which the shelter had been built, Karl had made a little cache of rocks behind the boulders, well above the creek's high water line, a little cairn marked with a bright red chunk of volcanic rock. In the cairn he had hidden the little hand ax, the enamelware dishes and the small amount of canned food. After leaving the spot where he had parted from Jerry, he had ridden straight to Wildcat Canyon, to find the cache unmolested, the food and other articles still there. He took the food, the ax and one cup, grimly relieved that Christy had not discovered the cairn.

He packed the food and the cup and ax into his saddle bags, along with the supply of food Parkin had placed there, rode out of the canyon on the disguised Bounce and started toward the slope that was favored by Ball. The sun was down and the sky rapidly growing dark long before he reached the place, but he kept steadily on. He needed no daylight to find the slope and valley stretch that was his objective. He let Bounce take his own time. Bounce had stood up to some hard grilling. He must turn the horse loose and catch up a new mount before he went on. It occurred to him that he might as well take Ball. Ball was as tough as Bounce, and certainly a great deal fresher.

The star-luminous sky was hung with the full late moon when Karl arrived at last at the slope he sought. He had advanced cautiously, keeping to cover all of the way. Barker Christy might be anywhere. Karl had learned long ago that one often finds things where one least expects them to be. He unsaddled Bounce and turned him loose, concealing his riding gear in a grotto-like space between several big pines where he had slept many times before. He lay down on the needle-covered earth, his saddle for a pillow, his saddle blanket sufficient covering against the slight chill of the night and early morning. He slept soundly, dreamlessly, and woke only when he heard two jays fighting in the trees above his head, woke to find the sky growing light.

He rose and got his breakfast, then went out to look for Ball. The dark brown horse with the four white stockings was feeding far up on the slope. Karl left him there, and began a methodical search for the place where the pinto must have been hidden. There were numerous places where a horse could have been con-cealed from all danger of chance detection, but in none of them was there any sign; no faint imprint, no

173

trampled ground, no shoe-grazed rocks, no heaped droppings. And in no spot but in some such thick cover would sign mean a thing, since horses were scattered all over the surrounding territory.

Karl was beginning to think he had guessed wide of the mark in his first attempt to follow Christy's moves. The crow told him differently. A very large crow, its feathers glinting in the early sun, rose from a spot among the heaped rocks that were strewn over a steep adjoining slope, a slope angling sharply upward from Ball's favorite feeding ground.

The crow had risen from the head of the thirty-foot high rubble heap. He rose cawing and flapping his wings noisily, and Karl turned quickly to gaze at him with narrowed eyes. He followed the flight of the carrion bird to a tall pine. Still cawing and gibbering, the crow lighted there.

Karl turned about on his heel, and stared up the rocky slope to the base of the wash. What had the crow been feasting on there? With a rapid stride, he crossed to the foot of the rubble heap, and scrutinized it closely. A man or a horse might get to the top of the heap without breaking a leg, but neither could go farther than the base of the wash. Karl's intent blue eyes studied the rubble. There was no sign to give him any clew. But something had gone up that slide of loose rock, had gone up and had not come down. He had heard that scolding cry of the crows too many times before not to know it.

Scrambling and leaning to the steep ascent, he

started making his way up the heap of rubble. The rocks slipped and rolled under his boots, allowing him only the poorest of footing. He consumed a good half hour in conquering the stubborn slope, but he finally reached the head of it and the foot of the wash. He looked about for some sign of the carrion upon which the crow had been feeding, and for a moment he saw nothing. Then his gaze lighted upon a heap of rock in the declivity made by the waters as they came dashing down to vent their fury on the rubble.

There was something unnatural about the heap. It had never been piled there by torrential waters. It had been piled by human hands. In a crevice between some of the stones there showed a patch of red and white. Karl cursed soundlessly under his breath and made his way with reckless speed to the heap of rock. He reached to pull aside some of the concealing stones. The red and white patch was pinto horse hide, and there was a gaping hole where the beak of a crow had torn at the edge of a wound around which the hair was stiffened with dried blood.

There was little need to expend the labor to uncover the carcass more, but Karl did it. He wanted to be certain, not merely to conjecture at the sight of a patch of hide. In a few moments he had removed enough rock to ascertain that beneath it lay a red and white pinto horse, branded on the shoulder with Christy's brand, the Circle C. The animal had been shot through the head. Karl rose slowly to his feet, tossing a few handfuls of rock back onto the exposed parts of the carcass.

Then he went back down the treacherous descent to the feeding ground below.

Karl laughed grimly to himself. "He's not so dumb. Too wise to keep going on that pinto. Forces him up that slope, shoots him, and buries him where there isn't once chance in a million of his being found. Turns Ball loose, steals one of our other horses and goes on. Hmm. Not so dumb! It isn't going to be any Sunday guessing game catching that hombre.

He went on across the feeding ground, his eyes searching for the horse he wanted for his own use. Ball had fed down the grassy slope until he had almost reached the bottom. Both Ball and Bounce had been taught from colthood to come when they were called. Karl walked toward the feeding horse, reaching into his pocket for a piece of bread he had put there for the purpose. Ball always expected to find something in an outstretched hand when he came in answer to a call. As Karl advanced to within a few yards of him, the horse raised his head and nickered.

Karl held out the piece of bread and whistled. Ball started toward him at a swinging walk, accepted the piece of bread amiably, and started toward the lower edge of the valley without protest, Karl's hand gripping his mane. Within a few moments, Ball was saddled and ready to ride, and Bounce, not recognizable to any man as Bounce till the paint wore off his legs and forehead, was left grazing and taking his ease in the valley.

One step at a time was sound premise, but a man

must know where to step next. Which way had Christy gone from there? He would not have gone north toward Heppner, too many ranches that way, too much danger of running into one of Lucky's or Chapman's cowboys. He might have gone west and south toward Sundown, had he been riding the pinto: no one would have thought much of seeing Bark Christy on a horse of his own, save to remark that he had come back again after several months' absence. That way, however, he might chance to meet any of two dozen different men from scattered ranches, any one of whom might think it decidedly queer for Barker Christy to be riding a Lazy S Block horse, when Christy was known to be violently disliked by the Sandses. He wouldn't risk it. Not when he was shrewd enough to get rid of the pinto. No, he wouldn't have gone south and west toward Sundown.

There remained but one direction in which he could have been likely to have fled: to the south and east, skirting the Lazy S, forging into the uninhabited fastnesses of the breaks towering along the Middle Fork of the John Day. Nobody lived over that way but a few isolated moonshiners.

In the early afternoon, Karl Sands drew rein before the thicket wherein Yude Tavistock's cabin was hidden. Fifty feet away you could not tell that a cabin was there unless you already knew it. Karl slipped out of the saddle and led Ball through the innocent-looking lane that led into the thicket, and came out into the little clearing before the cabin, which jutted hard against the slope rising behind it. Two goats lay in the shade of the thicket edge, half heartedly cropping the few leaves of brush within their reach. No other sign of life was about the cabin.

Karl left Ball standing, hidden in a brush clump, walked up to the door, which stood part way ajar, banged upon it lightly with his fist, and raised a hail.

"Hey, Yude! Come on out." For a moment there was no answering sound of any kind, then a slight murmur of lazy movement came to his ears, and Mrs. Tavistock appeared suddenly, as if she had been conjured there, beyond the opening of the door. She made no motion to open the portal wider, but stood there looking at Karl sleepily. Then a look of recognition crept into her eyes, and she spoke.

"Oh, it's you. Yude ain't here. He's up to the still. You know where it is, don't you?" Karl nodded, and the look in her eyes suddenly sharpened. She raised one hand to push back her disordered, dust-brown hair. "You better—oh, I guess it's all right. But he's kinda out of sorts. Better handle 'im easy." She turned and disappeared, as if she had said all there was to say.

Karl had a swift premonition that she was lying, that Yude was not up at the still, which was situated several rods from the cabin on a ledge back of another thicket on the slope to the right. He had a feeling that she was merely trying to get rid of him. She was too slow of wit to know how to lie easily and fluently. On the urge of an ungovernable impulse, he

178

shoved the door wide open and stepped into the cabin.

The woman, who had slumped into a broken down chair half way across the floor space, jerked upright, and stared at him with blank eyes. Yude lay on the bed against the wall beyond her, very still, his eyes closed, his face colorless. A bloody bandage was tied around his head. He was a very tall man, very thin, with a strikingly handsome head on his stick of a body. His finely cut nose and well shaped mouth were pinched, an odd look of drain and suffering was plain on every feature. He was breathing evenly and lightly. Otherwise, from the look of him, he might have been dead.

"What happened to him?" Karl asked quietly, discarding as an issue of no moment her lie about Yude being at the still.

Yude himself answered, before the woman had time to speak. His full, clearly gray eyes opened and turned in their sockets to fasten on Karl. "She talks too much for her own good," he said bluntly. "That's what happened."

Karl nodded, as if the whole matter were at once well explained, stepped to the tumbled bed and sat down at Yude's feet. "Sorry to see you knocked out, Yude. Anything I can do?"

Yude stared at him, his sharp gaze unblinking. "Yeh, there is. You can tell me what the hell your hired man's doin' runnin' over the country knockin' people out *for.*"

Karl's eyes veiled. "Sure he was one of our men, Yude?"

"Ridin' one of your horses," Yude answered curtly. "Ridin' that big roan with the black mane and tail that you had over here one day. He seen the missus out gittin' wood to cook supper and followed her to the house. I had him spotted long before he got here. Knowed the roan. Didn't think nothin' of it. Every once in a while some of you fellas gits over here. Always kind of glad to see 'em. Git some news from outside." To Yude and his clan, the world beyond the isolated fastness of the breaks was "outside." Yude's clear gray eyes hardened slightly, and a queer furtive look of sudden fear crossed his handsome face. "Who is that damn fool, anyhow? Some new man you got?"

"He wasn't one of our men, whoever he was." Karl chose his words with caution. "None of our boys has been over this way in months, I happen to know that. Whoever was riding that roan stole it."

Yude sat up in bed abruptly, swaying dizzily, shooting a strange look at his wife. Didn't I tell yuh? Damn him! He— Yude cut himself short, and the look of furtive fear bloomed for a moment into an expression of abject terror.

"What did he do?" Karl demanded, his gaze boring into Yude's whitened face. "What's the matter with you, Yude? I never knew you to be afraid of hell and high water."

"Who said I was afraid of anything?" Yude snapped, and hunched himself up in a crouching position, against the head of the bed.

"Your face said it." Karl held him to gaze mercilessly. "Spit it out. What the hell happened over here, anyway?"

"I ain't tellin'," Yude answered, his voice thick. He turned his gaze on his wife, who sat staring at him in something of the same terror that had lately lighted his own face. "And you keep your mouth shut too, old woman, or it'll be the worse for yuh! You don't know what he was talkin' about, but I do. Keep your mouth shut! You hear?" She nodded, swiftly, as if it were a great effort. "Well, see that you do it, then," Yude growled, and turned his attention back to Karl. "You ain't gittin' nothin' outa me, so you might as well beat it," he snapped. "Maybe he was one of your men, and maybe he wasn't. Said he was. Anyway, he comes back here and I'll kill him like I would a rattler. I'd a killed him this time, only he was too damn quick for me."

Karl rose to his feet, reluctant to give up questioning Yude, but realizing that such a procedure was quite useless. "Which way did he go?" he asked.

"How the hell do I know?" Yude sneered. "I was knocked out cold. Wonder he didn't kill me. Reckon he tried to, all right."

The woman started to speak. "He went—"

"Shut up!" roared Yude. "Want to git your fool brains blowed out? You don't know, any more'n I do. He went, and that's enough."

Karl stood for a moment in silence, gazing intently at the man on the bed. What was Yude afraid of? It would have needed something of moment, and something personally threatening, to instill Yude with that open terror. People here knew little about Yude Tavistock. He kept to himself and the inhabitants of the mountains let him alone, as he obviously wanted to be let alone. No one knew where he had come from, and no one knew what his former life had been. A man usually did not show that kind of fear unless there was something he did not want known, and he was well aware that some one knew it and was in terror lest others learn it.

Karl frowned down at Tavistock, thinking swiftly. Had it been Christy on the roan? Had Christy by some unholy chance known Tavistock in some other place, and had he known something that had taken place there which Yude had tried to leave behind? It was a reasonable supposition. Karl sat down upon the bed again.

"Listen here, Yude. Let me talk for a few minutes, and you keep still. When I get through you may be more willing to talk. I'm looking for a man who has stolen one of our horses. He killed Frank's wife and shot Frank. Blinded Frank. Everything conspires to point at me as the killer. If I don't find the man who did it and take him in and prove that I had nothing to do with it, it looks just black enough for me that I'll have to keep going—and not come back. Even Frank thinks I did it. Now, you get your head to working and come out of it. This fellow who came over here on the roan may be the man I'm looking for. I want to know what you know about him."

Yude's face was utterly without expression, there was nothing more to be read on his colorless features than there is on the blank wall of a house. "I hope yuh find him, but I ain't got nothin' to tell."

A low, long-drawn whistle penetrated into the sudden silence that filled the small room. Karl heard Yude's wife emit a sudden startled exclamation, but he held his gaze intently on the man on the bed. Tavistock betrayed no expression, but Karl knew that he was annoyed. Mrs. Tavistock started to rise from her chair, but Yude's voice stopped her.

"Siddown! Siddown and stay there. Don't you dare go to the door. This place is too damn popular of a sudden. Shut that door, Karl, and keep still. Somebody's comin'. Hell! I wonder if that fool'd dare to come back here!" He sat erect, his face set, his emaciated body shivering in sheer fear. "Shut that door, quick!"

Karl rose and crossed the floor in long soundless strides. He closed the door and returned to his seat at the foot of the bed. "Who whistled?" he asked in a barely audible undertone.

"Kinney," Yude answered in whisper. "He's been back for a month. Shut up, will yuh?"

Kinney Tavistock was Yude's twin brother, but the two looked no more alike than if they had been no relation to each other. Kinney was thin, there lay the only resemblance. He was little over five feet tall, lean and ugly, straw-red hair, white lashes and brows, florid freckled skin and great hamlike hands on thin spindling arms. He got around through the forest and the thickets like a deer, went up the rocky slopes like a goat. He was Yude's lookout and go-between, went on regular trips to the outside to sell Yude's whiskey, and not ten people living in the mountains ever saw him from one year's end to another.

Part of Yude's Argus-eyed watch of the surrounding territory was due to Kinney. That there was any signal between the two by which one warned the other of the approach of anyone Karl had not known. He sat motionless on the foot of the bed, watching Yude and waiting.

But Yude had slipped into unconsciousness and was breathing harshly. The ugly gash in his head was bleeding again.

Karl turned to the woman with a frown of anxiety. "Bring me some water and some cloths. He's burning up with a fever. I can't leave him like this."

"He was havin' a fever all night." The woman rose, moving sluggishly, with no change of expression. "He won't let nobody do nothin'."

"He won't know anything about it." Karl restrained his impatience with the woman, and glanced down at Tavistock. "He's clean out. Hurry! That's a nasty crack he got on his head."

The woman moved across the floor on leaden feet, as if all hope had gone from her life years since, as if there were nothing to move for. From the pail on a bench in the corner at the other end of the room, she poured some water into a pan, water that had grown tepid in the all pervading heat of the sun. She picked up a grimy rag of a much washed meal sack lying on one end of the bench, tore it in two, and carried rag and basin to Karl. Karl glanced at the soiled rag, thrust one finger into the tepid water, and muttered an impatient curse.

"That's too warm. I'll get some from the creek." He took the basin and was gone from the room before the woman could utter the remonstrance formulating on her tongue.

He hurried across the clearing, through the lane and to the slope to the left, where a small spring farther up the canyon sent a small creek purling down. He emptied the basin and dipped up a panful of the cold water, retraced his steps to the cabin and started across the room to bathe the injured man's face and brow. But he stopped short in the middle of a stride.

Yude Tavistock was gone. He was not on the bed, and he was not anywhere in the room. The woman stood against the wall, staring at Karl with frightened eyes.

"I told you he wouldn't let nobody do nothin' for him. You git out! You git out right now! The minute you was out of the room, he crawled off the bed and followed you. He's mad, and he's scared. You go, now!"

On the heels of her half-imploring, half-demanding speech, the low long-drawn whistle came again from somewhere up on the slope of one of the three surrounding mountains. In an instant it was repeated, twice.

"My God!" the woman gasped. "There's more of 'em comin'! Two of 'em this time. Git out, you!" The command was frantic with fear. "Git out and keep goin'!"

"All right, I'm going!" Karl sat down the basin on the rough table against the wall within a yard of him, then turned to bend a searching gaze on her face. "But if that fellow comes back here, the one who cracked Yude on the head, you tell him I was here. He thought it was I he was shooting when he shot Frank. You tell him he didn't get me, and I'm on his trail."

"You're crazy!" the woman gasped. "You're plumb crazy! He'll sneak right over there to the Lazy S after yuh."

"I hope so!" Karl retorted savagely. "That may be the only way I'll ever get him. You tell him, if he ever comes back. You tell Yude to tell him! I'm gone."

He flashed out of the door before the woman could call after him, dashed across the clearing and out through the lane cut through the thicket. He retrieved Ball from the brush where he had hidden him, and retreated to a concealing cover down the canyon from the hidden clearing. There he again left Ball, and crawled a few yards up the steep slope, to a spot from which he could command a view of the canyon and the approach of the thicket within which the cabin was built.

6

CROUCHED MOTIONLESS in the brush, Karl heard a shrill whistle rise from the clearing in the thicket, a whistle that was blended of three short blasts of sound. It was answered from somewhere upon the slope above him, by the same whistle he had heard when he was in the room with Yude and the woman. Then silence again, and in the distance in the same direction from which he himself had come, he saw two men approaching on horses. A barely audible slithering sound passed him in the brush, and in the next moment Kinney emerged into view, running toward the thicket which hid the house, and disappeared into the lane. Evidently either Yude or the woman had called him in.

The two horsemen drew near rapidly, and Karl saw that they were cowboys, one from the Double Luck ranch and one from Chapman's. Before they could reach the lane through the thicket, Kinney emerged again and came to meet them.

Gister, the man from Chapman's, pulled up his horse and remained in the saddle. The Double Luck cowboy, Ed Martin, dismounted and spoke brusquely to Kinney.

"Hello, Kinney. You seen any suspicious lookin' fellas over this way?"

Kinney yawned. "Uh uh. Nobody ever comes over this way. Who you lookin' fer?"

"Rustlers," Martin returned succinctly. "We caught 'em in the act, but they got away from us, and they sure did come this way. Strangers to us. Little skinny guy about your size, with black angora chaps on, and a big fat fella."

"Ain't see nobody," Kinney asserted with indolent indifference. "If I do see 'em I'll stop 'em. Come to think of it," he added cautiously, "I did see one of the Lazy S boys ridin' over here to see Yude. That's all, though."

"Oh, that's nothing to do with this," Martin answered, turning to his horse and getting back into the saddle. "They re probably looking for the same fellas we are. We been missin' a good bit of stuff, and the boss is gettin' damn sick of it. Funny them fellas would have headed over this way. One of 'em just about your size."

"Say! Kinney bristled. "You ain't accusin' *me* of rustlin' nobody's cows, are yuh?"

"Why, no!" Martin's surprise was as genuine as his denial of any such thought. "What do you want of cows?"

Karl, impelled by a grim determination to take advantage of every least opportunity presented to him, suddenly raised to his feet and called down the slope.

"Hey, Ed! You and Giss wait a minute!"

They turned in their saddles to stare up at him in astonishment, as he came crashing through the brush down the slope toward them. Kinney yawned again and barely gave Karl the merest glance. Gister and

Martin exchanged puzzled, surprised glances, then sat lounging in their saddles, waiting Karl's approach. When he was within normal speaking distance, Martin addressed him with dry sarcasm.

"What do you think you're doin'? Givin' yourself up again?"

"I'm giving you and Giss credit for a little brains," Karl snapped, coming to a halt beside the horses. "I'm after Bark Christy, and I'm setting the cactus telegraph to work to find him. I didn't do that shooting, and if you had any sense you'd know it. Christy did, and I'm after him. How far are you going back this way?"

Martin shrugged and raised his eyebrows. "Damned if I know. Till we're sure we can't find no trace of them rustlers, that's sure. Why?"

"You tell everybody you see back in the mountains that Christy tried to get me and didn't, and that I'm back on the Lazy S laying for him."

"Yeah?" Martin laughed. "And who the hell do you think we're gonna see back in the mountains?"

"How do I know?" Karl frowned, impatient with Martin's levity. "Some of the moonshiners, maybe. Who the hell would have thought that I'd see you over here today?"

"I guess that's right," Martin conceded. "Well, I ain't messin' in nobody's shootin' scrapes. If you did do that shootin' over on the Lazy S you'll never git out of the mountains with all the country on the lookout for you. If you didn't do it, I don't know as I'd want to remember that I didn't lend a hand for you when I had a chance. Yeh, anybody I see I'll tell 'em that. Don't know as it's necessary, though. Kinney knows it."

Kinney grinned. "Yeah. Half the fellas in the hills'll know it afore sundown."

Martin and Gister started to turn away, then Martin suddenly looked back and called over his shoulder. "By the way, where the hell *will* you be, in case a fella wants to git some word to you?"

"On the Lazy S," Karl answered. "Laying for Christy."

Martin and Gister went on, and Karl turned to Kinney. The little man's ugly face was a blank, his cat-like eyes were watching Karl with a lazy stare.

"Do you know Bark Christy?" Karl asked.

"Heard of him," Kinney admitted. "Never seen him."

"Who cracked Yude on the head?"

Kinney's lazy stare grew vague. "Ask Yude."

Karl turned on his heel and strode toward the brush clump where Ball waited him. Another thought had come into his head a few moments since that would bear a little study. It had come when Kinney bristled and asked Martin if he was accusing him of rustling anybody's cows. Manifestly, Kinney couldn't have been the man Martin and Gister had seen branding calves, or whatever it was they had caught them doing. But Kinney had been just a little bit too indignant at the idea of anyone taking him for a rustler. Just as indignant as a rustler, a very shrewd rustler, might act were he caught off guard for a second.

As Karl rode away from the canyon and took his direction toward the long range of breaks running down the Middle Fork, he was thinking as hard as he had ever thought in his life. Seeking Christy, he had come upon two other issues, and he had a sure instinct that they were in some way joined together. It was not fear of Christy personally that had about demoralized Yude Tavistock (for Karl was inwardly certain that the man on the roan had been Christy), it was fear of something Christy knew.

"And the more I think of it," Karl told himself with positive conviction, "it isn't anything that happened a long time ago, either. It's something that's going on right now. Though what happened in Idaho years ago may be mixed up in it. That look on Yude's face. Hell, the man was scared within an inch of his life."

Karl frowned and shook his head, like a man trying to clear his sight, as Ball carefully took his way along the faint tortuous trail hugging the slope of the break he was slowly ascending. Yude wasn't the only one who was frightened. The woman was on the edge of a panic. Kinney himself, behind that sleepy ugly mask of a face, was as much on edge as a man one jump ahead of the hangman's noose. And Kinney knew something about the rustling going on. Yude and Kinney perhaps. Maybe they brought in stolen stuff a few head at a time and Christy received it and disposed of it, dividing the profits.

Karl felt a tingle of excitement as he saw the pieces begin to fit together. Such a scheme would be almost air-tight, probably had been in operation right there under the ranchers' noses for years. Christy's ranch was pretty well off to itself, and he kept such small herds that he was considered of no consequence in the affairs of the cattle country. Yude and Kinney could have gotten away with a thing like that almost too easily. Nobody paid much attention to the moonshiners and their spasmodic comings and goings. Yude's protestations that the man on the roan was a stranger amounted to precisely nothing. The woman's declarations amounted to no more. Probably she was a better liar than he had thought, Karl admitted to himself.

The more he considered the supposition, the more probable it grew. He backed Ball from the rim onto the dry grass stretch of the terrace, still frowning and trying to decide on the wisest move to make next. If Yude and Kinney were stealing cattle and turning them over to Christy, they would have some retreat where they cached them till they were ready to move them. This being the strategic time to gather in a few head, before the fall roundup, they would have some cattle held in that hideout. They were not working alone, since Martin and Gister had come upon those two who were following, the little man about Kinney's size and the big fat fellow.

"That would be five of them," Karl mused. "Those two, the Tavistock twins, and Christy. Probably no

192

more. That's enough to keep a secret dark. More would be too dangerous. But who in hell are the little skinny man and the big fat fellow?"

The far-flung breaks, rising majestic in the sun, could give him no answer. He raised his gaze to the plateau edge across the river where the wild horses were disappearing. Wild horses and wild breaks. They belonged together. What was there about those wild horses disappearing onto that high plateau that gave him a sudden idea? Since he could remember he had ridden the breaks, he had loved them and studied them tirelessly, they were a part of life. Always there had been wild horses. But there was something about these horses that had caught his attention.

Then his wandering brain focused and he knew what it was. Those horses were not traveling in the carefree manner of wild horses looking for forage or moving to another feeding ground because the notion had suddenly struck them: they were moving like animals suddenly startled, uneasy. They were moving because they had seen or scented something that warned them of an enemy presence and urged them to get away from it. And what was the enemy presence most likely to startle wild horses on the breaks? Man.

Karl nudged Ball into motion and turned to an angling course toward the foot of the break he had started to climb, toward that region of slope that descended to the river. He forded the river and rode on with all possible speed to the break up which the wild horses had gone. He ascended it to the point where he had first seen the wild horses in motion, and brought Ball to a halt. Careful scrutiny showed him that no one was in sight anywhere. He had but one guide, the faint wind. He looked closely at the branches of the trees. The wind that must have carried the scent to the wild horses was too sluggish to move even the boughs of the trees. He could not determine its direction by them.

"Well, other things besides straws tell the way the wind blows," he said to Ball grimly.

He drew papers and tobacco from his pocket, rolled a cigarette and lighted it. He returned papers and tobacco to his pocket, and held the cigarette away from him, watching it sharply. The smoke from its tip twisted like an unfurling sail, away to the west. The scent had come to the animals from the east. He cocked the corker of his cigarette in the corner of his mouth and rode down the break to the east. He was traveling directly toward the Circle C, Christy's ranch.

He rode slowly, cautiously, keeping continually under cover. He descended from the break to the long twisting canyon that stretched away from it before he saw or heard a thing to tell him that his course had been leading toward any real objective. Within a few rods of the foot of the break, down the deep canyon, he saw two men moving at an indolent pace, as if they had quite all eternity to reach whatever place they were going to. One was a small, very thin man, just about the size of Kinney Tavistock. He wore flapping black angora chaps. The other was a big fat man on a sorrel. Before them plodded nine head of very young, very fine beef cattle.

Karl smiled to himself, and crushed out his cigarette stub on the horn of his saddle. If those cattle hadn't come from Lucky's ranch, he was willing to quit handling cattle. He knew. Two of them were from among the yearlings he had sold Lucky the day he had found Floria in Wildcat Canyon. The other seven were younger, too young as yet to have felt the branding iron. Men and stolen cattle were traveling rather carefully, yet it was easy to see that the men were confident of their safety in isolation. Karl nudged Ball into motion again, keeping to cover even more scrupulously than he had done before.

The sun set west of the high breaks and pinnacles before he found out. The men drove the cattle down the canyon till they came to a branching side canyon. The main canyon branched to the south here and the side canyon continued to the east. The men drove the cattle down the side canyon. Slightly over a half mile along the smaller canyon they came to a stout brush corral. In the enclosure were twenty-three other cattle, easily discerned in the twilight. The nine head were driven in with the twenty-three and the corral closed. Karl sat his saddle in the cover of firs and pines and watched.

The men did not dismount, but sat their saddles and glanced frequently up the slope to the north, evidently waiting the coming of someone else. Before the dark had fallen the third man came, and Karl swore in delight at developments taking place before his eyes. The third man was Barker Christy, on the Lazy S roan with the black mane and tail.

"How many did you git this haul?" Christy asked, without troubling to look in the corral and count them. His voice carried clearly in the mountain air.

"Nine," said the big fat fellow on the sorrel. "Two of 'em branded. Double Luck stuff this trip."

"Damn it, why *will* you risk bringing in the branded stuff?" Christy complained. "You got a branded two-year-old in the Chapman bunch, and I warned you then. You damned fools will break my neck yet."

"Oh, don't you go gittin' het up, Bark," protested the little man in the black angora chaps. "Three ain't bad. I can git rid of that much beef without half tryin'. Finner was askin' for some more of our stuff a couple of weeks ago."

"Well, Finner ain't gittin' it," snapped Christy. "You're turnin' them three out and takin' 'em back across the river tomorrow. I'm done in this man's country. I'm gittin' out."

"Huh! Done?"

'Gittin' out?" The two exclamations of astonishment came in one breath.

"That's what I said." Christy's face was ugly in the thickening dusk. "It ain't none of your business why, only this much: there's been too much damn talk about missin' cattle from the Chapman outfit and from Tom Lucky's cowboys. Our easy pickin's are finished. When the country begins to talk about it, it's time to

196

pull your freight. If you ain't got sense enough to take the warning and light out, you're due to be chief guest at a necktie party. None of that in mine."

"Hell!" Karl could no longer distinguish the three men, the dusk was deepening so rapidly, but he was certain that the angry expletive had come from the fat man. The disgruntled rustler began to expostulate. "Let 'em talk. We're safe as long as they don't do nothin' but talk."

"Well, they're doin' more! Don't argue with me!" Christy was out of all patience on the instant. "A couple of men from the Double Luck and the Bar C Bar followed you as far as the moonshiner's this afternoon. I saw 'em, and I hightailed it right after 'em to see what they were up to. I couldn't get near enough to see what went on, didn't dare. But they rode into his canyon, and pretty soon I saw 'em come out again. I beat it, without wastin' time."

"Hell, we didn't go to the moonshiner's," protested the fat man.

"You went in that direction till you forded the river," Christy countered. "And that was enough. They got your drift, and must have gone on over there to see what they could find out. That's too damn close for me."

"Close my eye!" The little man put in. "The moonshiner ain't got nothing to do with us. He don't know nothing that could do us any damage."

Christy laughed, a short sneering sound that carried meaning to only one man within hearing distance, to

Karl Sands. "All the moonshiners know too damn much for their own health," Christy retorted. "Shut up and stop arguin'. I'm tellin' you what to do and you're doin' it. You take those three branded critters back over the river tomorrow, and turn 'em loose. Drive the rest of 'em down to the corral on my place and leave 'em. I'll take care of 'em later. You're gittin' paid off and you're gittin' out!"

"When?"

"Day after tomorrow, and not a minute later. And don't you forget it."

"But what are you goin'—"

"What I'm going to do is none of your damned business. You do as I say and be at the ranch with the stuff not later than sundown, day after tomorrow. I'll be there waitin' for you. We've got to move. This time next week I'll be a long way from here, and so will you if you want to keep your heads on."

Christy rode away without another word, and Karl heard the sound of his departing horse's hoof beats. The other two men evidently intended to remain where they were for the night. From their disgruntled talk it became clear to the motionless listener that they were dismounting and making preparations to build a fire and get a meal.

Karl decided that it was time for him to move, also. He must reach the ranch and return with some of the boys before these two in the canyon got away with the cattle. He hadn't too many hours at his command. He led Ball cautiously away from the spot where he had been watching and listening to the men below, forced to take a snail's pace lest by the least haste he make some sound that would apprise the rustlers of his presence. He consumed nearly an hour in withdrawing far enough from them that he felt it safe to mount Ball and make speed.

He never knew that, as he made his slow and careful way from the canyon, a man, lying hidden but a little distance from him, rose to his feet and slipped off through the shadows as silently as any cat of the forest. A very small man, thin, approximately the same size as the smaller man in the canyon. He struck off down the canyon, to follow and overtake Barkcr Christy. Had the night not hidden him, one might have been able to discern that the small brown pony he rode bore the Circle C, Christy's brand, and that the small man's ugly face was hideous with anger and malevolent scheming.

Karl reached the river and forded it under the light of the lazy moon and the winking stars. He could reach the ranch by daylight, if he traveled steadily. He would get Bass Todd and Clink Lafferty and Bert Gray. He regretted a great deal the shortness of time given him, since it allowed him no opportunity to ride on to the Double Luck or the Bar C Bar and bring men from there, to catch the rustlers red-handed, to prove before all of them the guilt of Barker Christy and to exonerate himself. His blond young face was bitten deep by the lines that nothing could ever erase, the lines of bitterness and pain the last few days had etched on his features.

And while he rode steadily onward, engrossed by his plans and his bitter thoughts, the little man who had gone down the canyon on the brown pony was making quite as good time on his errand.

The man on the brown pony followed the canyon for a mile or more, then took a course to the south, across a long low ridge, along another canyon, and finally drew rein in a small flat among the ever-present thickets in the bed of the second canyon. Standing forlornly at one side of the flat, clearly revealed in the moonlight, was a dilapidated line cabin, long since abandoned by the cowboys who had once ridden there in past years. The roof was sagging, the rough boards that composed the sides were warped and split. There was nothing to tell that anyone had been near the place in a decade—save a little chink of dim light showing at the bottom of a heavy sack nailed over the one window at the side.

The small man slipped off the brown pony, dropped its reins, and uttered the same long low whistle that Karl had heard that afternoon in the moonshiner's cabin. After a moment of silence that seemed to have an oddly startled air, the whistle was repeated from within the old line cabin. The little man left the brown pony, strode swiftly to the tightly closed old door, swung it open a little way and slipped inside the room, pulling the door again swiftly shut.

Inside the cabin, beside an old table made of two

200

planks and held up by blocks of wood since its legs were long since gone, Barker Christy sat on another block of wood, counting a small heap of money by the light of a candle stuck into a rusted old tin can. He looked up with an inquiring frown, as the small man paused a few feet from him.

"What the hell do *you* want?" Christy snapped.

The small man's gash of a mouth quirked in a derisive grin. One ham-like hand raised to rumple his disordered straw-red hair. His white eyebrows raised, his yellowish eyes mocking beneath them. "It ain't what I want that's brought me here. It's what Karl Sands wants."

Christy started, paled, then sat utterly still, staring at the small man with protruding eyes. "You're crazy!" His voice was hoarse with consternation. "What're you tryin' to hand me, you double-crossin' fool? Karl Sands is as dead as last year's mutton! What's the matter with your ears? Hadn't you heard that?"

Kinney Tavistock's grin grew to an open sneer. "No, I hadn't heard it. Where'd *you* hear it?"

Christy shifted uneasily on his block of wood. "Why, you poor fool, it's all over the country. Everybody knows it. I heard it in Sundown, myself."

"You ain't been in Sundown." Kinney licked his lips, with the avid wolfish expression of a coyote surveying a carcass with watering mouth. His white-lashed lids blinked rapidly, as if they would hide the gleam in his cat-yellow eyes. "That's once you slipped, Bark! You had it on me, all right! I'd never have had anything to do with your rustlin' scheme if you hadn't threatened to turn me in for killin' that crook in Idaho. But I've got it on you, now, damn yuh! I only killed a man that needed killin'! You killed a woman! You blinded a man that's a damn good man, Frank Sands. Blinded him, yuh hear? I got you where I want you, now!"

"You're lyin'!" Christy swayed to his feet, his face pasty, his features working till his countenance was rendered a horrid writhing mask. "You're tryin' to get my goat! You're lyin'! It couldn't a been Frank! You're crazy! It was Karl!"

"It was Frank," Kinney reiterated. He was gloating, openly, savoring his triumph to the full over the man who had persecuted him. "Karl's a damn live corpse, right there on the Lazy S. I seen him with my own eyes, ridin' along the ridge this side of the ranch."

Christy drew a deep breath, expelled it in a blast, and slowly sank down on the block of wood. "If you're tellin' me the truth, we'd better talk turkey. If you're lyin' to me, God help your soul!"

"I ain't lyin'." Kinney's face was openly contemptuous as he sat down upon a battered old crate, facing Christy. "But I'm damn glad I got you where you'll have to keep your mouth shut. So far as the rest of it's concerned, there's one thing you got to do before we light out of here. You *got* to get Karl now, or there's no chance for you."

"You tellin' me?" Christy laughed, a short ugly laugh of derision. "I'll get him, and this time there'll be no mistake about it. But you've got to help me."

"Oh, I'll help you." Kinney shrugged. "What do you think I'm here for? But then I'm done with yuh. You hear? You go your way and I'm goin' mine. I'll help yuh get Karl Sands, but you'll do the shootin'! I ain't forgittin' what a skunk you've been, not now or any time! Why didn't you let Yude alone?"

Christy laughed. "Why didn't Yude let me alone? I didn't do a damn thing but ride up there and ask for you. He didn't recognize me, he thought I was one of the Lazy S men. He coulda gone on thinkin' so if he hadn't got fresh with me."

Kinney's ugly face twisted, his yellow eyes burned with a dangerous light. "You lowdown liar! He didn't get fresh with anybody. He only said I wasn't there. I'd told him to say it."

"Well, that's where *you* slipped," sneered Christy. "I had to get hold of you, and I had to bring him to time some way."

But you needn't have told him I was helpin' yuh sneak the Double Luck and Bar C Bar cattle, damn yuh!"

Again Christy laughed. "And he needn't have called me a filthy liar for it. If he'd been civil I wouldn't a clouted him one."

Kinney's twisted face chilled, the color faded from it so that the freckles stood out even in the light of the candle in the old rusted can. "You nearly did for him with that crack, but he's gittin' over it. He's too tough to die from a scratch like that. But he didn't believe what you said about me rustlin', and I denied it. He's goin' to keep on not believin' it! He's scared stiff for fear you'll let it out about that fuss in Idaho and git my neck stretched. But I finally got him persuaded that you'll keep your mouth shut—because I've finally got one on you. You see where I got you, don't yuh? All right, then. You talk turkey, and you talk fast."

Christy sat motionless on the block of wood, slowly stuffing into his pockets the small amount of bills he had been counting. His face was expressionless in the candle light, but somehow inexpressibly repellent and evil, all its superficial good looks marred. His finely built body was relaxed, like the body of a cat making ready to tense for a leap on some unsuspecting prey. Suddenly he lifted his gaze to Kinney's yellow eyes and laughed.

"I guess we're quits," he admitted grimly. "Let it go at that. Where's that Sands kid now?"

Kinney frowned. "On his way home, I guess. He was there at Yude's cabin when you followed Ed Martin and Lew Gister as far as yuh dared. He was talkin' to Ed and Giss. He's tellin' everybody that he knows you done the shootin' on the Lazy S Block and he's layin' for yuh there. He told Ed and Giss that. Then he got his horse and beat it. I followed him. He come moseyin' over this way and ran smack into Bat and Loozey, sat there on his horse and listened to all that went on between you and Bat and Loozey, then he went back the way he come. Gone to the Lazy S to git some of the boys and round up the outfit, of course."

Christy sat erect, his eyes widening in dismay. "Hell! We got to stop that! We got to beat him there somehow and shut his mouth before he tells what he's found out!"

"Keep your hair on! Keep your hair on!" Kinney's ugly face twisted into a hundred lines of evil cunning. "Let him go and git 'em on the track! What the hell do we care what happens to Bat and Loozey so long as we git clear?"

"Yeh, I guess that's right," Christy conceded, relaxing again.

"Well, use your head, then. Now see here." Kinney leaned forward confidentially. "You and me *got* to work together now. Neither of us can afford to doublecross the other. For the safety of us both, we got to git Karl Sands! Agreed?"

Christy raised amused brows. "You think I don't know it?"

"All right, then, listen. I got it all doped out. Slick as grease. It can't fail. Karl's gone to the ranch for help, as sure as you're a foot high. All right. Let the fool go. We'll mosey over there ourselves, and cache ourselves where we can get a look-in. When he takes the boys and starts out to follow Bat and Loozey, I'll follow him. Before he gets very far, I'll ride out and show myself and get him aside. Nobody'll think anything of seein' me anywhere. I can always say I just got back from Heppner, or anything else that comes handy. Nobody's got the least suspicion of me yet."

"So far so good," Christy put in dryly, "but I don't get your drift."

"You will in a minute." Kinney's evil eyes leered yellow in the dim candle glow. "I'll tell Karl I got something special to tell him. Then I'll whisper it to him that you're on your way to the Lazy S lookin' for him, and tell him he better send the other fellows on without him if he wants to git a lick at you. He'll do it, yuh needn't doubt that."

A slow smile began to grow on Christy's face. "I think I'm about two jumps ahead of you."

"Maybe." The sinister smile was reflected for a moment on Kinney's ugly features. "I'll git him back to the Lazy S, and tell him I'm gonna lead him to your hideout. Once I git him there, you can do the rest."

"And him the best shot in the John Day?" Christy snapped. "What kind of a fool do you think I am, to go up against that hombre in a gun fight?"

Kinney smirked. "You ain't got the best part of it yet. You're goin' to be cached right there by the barn. I'll stall around, some way or other, and manage to git hold of his gun. I'll git him right out where he'll be a fair target, and you can take him down without half tryin'. If you miss the first shot, like you missed when you took a pot at Frank, he won't have no gun and you can get him with the second." He leered at the staring Christy. Air tight, ain't it?"

Christy pursed his lips, frowning. "Yeah, I guess it is. But how you goin' to do all that?"

"I don't know yet: But you know me. I'll do it. I'll

do it, and he'll never have a smell of a suspicion of what I'm up to. Well, what about it?"

"Good enough." Christy rose briskly to his feet. "I kinder hate to give up the little handful I'd be gittin' for the herd Bat and Loozey are takin' in, but it can't be helped. I don't want none of what Bat and Loozey are goin' to get. Go on out, and I'll be with you in a minute."

Kinney nodded, rose from the old crate, and went out of the room without a backward look. He had no least fear that Christy would put a bullet between his shoulder blades as he went. Christy needed him. He had told the truth. Neither of them could afford to doublecross the other.

He walked over to his brown pony, hoisted himself into the saddle and sat waiting patiently for Christy to put in an appearance. He hadn't long to wait. Christy came riding across the flat in the moonlight, on the roan with the black mane and tail, and the two started off together, bound for the Lazy S Block ranch.

The first faint light of daybreak was brushing the sky when Karl rode out of the cottonwoods onto the flat by the river. Before he went into the house, he decided to have a fresh horse ready to ride. He unsaddled Ball and turned him loose on the flat below the barn, carried his riding gear to the barn and went in to get another mount. He came out leading a tall rangy horse that was a cross between a dun and a roan, an animal of nondescript color but of great power and endurance. He saddled the animal, long ago named Dirty by the boys, and left him waiting by the corral. Then he went on to the house with long purposeful strides.

No one was up anywhere as yet, but the boys would be piling out within another half hour. Karl went up the back steps, opened the kitchen door, and stepped softly into the house. Profound silence reigned around him. He crossed the living room and quietly opened his father's door. Sands was asleep, his bandaged face turned slightly toward the door. Karl remained motionless for a moment, staring down at him, swept and shaken by an uncontrollable sweep of emotion. Then he set himself against that flood of memories, and stepped to the bedside. He laid a hand on his father's hand, lying against the quilt, gripped it tightly.

Frank stirred, turned his head, then sat up in bed quickly, as if something had stung him awake. He returned the grip on the hand that held his, then the grip loosened and his face quivered, then went still.

"Karl! It can't be—Karl?"

"Yes." Karl sat down on the edge of the bed. "I've found Christy, Frank."

Sands caught his breath sharply, wincing as if it hurt him. "You've found Christy!" he echoed.

"Yes. I had a cold trail to follow, and it looked damned hopeless, but I caught up with him last night. It's Christy and some other fellows who've been taking cattle from Lucky and Chapman and the other ranchers around here. The Tavistock twins are mixed up in it some way. I learned that much, then I came back for help. I'm after some of the boys to go with me and round 'em up. I know just where to get 'em red-handed in less than twenty-four hours."

Sands reached out a groping hand. The reaching fingers touched Karl's arm, and gripped there. He sat before his son, a stern and upright figure in the dim morning light, more gaunt than he had ever been before. Since he had been wounded he had lost many pounds, and suffering from his physical pain was least of the causes. He tried twice to speak, but the words seemed fast in his throat, then he managed his voice at last, with tremendous effort.

"Karl. You are still my son. If you have borrowed my blood, you couldn't lie. Why are you making such a play as this—if you can't prove what you have said?"

"I *can* prove it," Karl said steadily.

"But if that is so—I have to believe you, and have to condemn her as something unspeakable. And I can't! I can't!"

"Who do you want to believe?" Karl's voice shook.

"You!" Sands' cry reached into the next room. "I want to believe you! Go get Christy—so that I can believe what I want to believe, that she lied! Go get him!"

"I'm going." Karl sprang to his feet, and his hand gripped tensely for a space on his father's shoulder. As he went out the door, he said to himself under his breath—"He believes already, only he doesn't know it." Then before him he saw Jeudi. She had come out of her room, the room that had been his, his old sweater over her night gown.

"Karl! I heard you talking to father!"

Karl stood rooted. "My God, Judy! I'd forgotten!" He reached her in one long stride, his arms went around her. "What did he say?"

"Oh, he was glad! Awfully glad!" Jeudi looked up with her black eyes shining. "He said he'd always known, only he hadn't known what it was he knew. He—he really believes in you right now, only he doesn't know that, either."

"He will know it, before long!" Karl released her and gestured toward the outer door. "I have to go, Judy. I have to get the boys and make a roundup that's going to jar the whole John Day country. Keep him believing, till I come back."

He was gone out the door, afraid to remain, as Frank Sands came from his bedroom in stocking feet, calling for Jeudi. By the time Karl reached the bunkhouse to rouse the men, Sands had told her all Karl said. Gray and Riceman popped up in their beds like jack-in-the-box men as Karl stamped in, calling them awake. Within the next few minutes every man was up and listening, and Karl realized by the way they gazed at him that they only half believed what he was saying.

"Snap out of it,' he commanded sharply. "I don't give a damn whether you believe in me or not, or what crazy idea you have of any motive I could have had in committing such an act. All I want is for you to crawl out of this and get your horses. I've got a line on the rustlers, I tell you, and we haven't any time to lose if we're going to get them. Bert, I want you and Clink and Bass, as quick as you can shake some life into your carcasses."

"You'll get more than that!" Riceman informed him, leaping out of bed and reaching for his clothes. "Every damn man of us'll see this through. I'm beginning to think there may be something in it."

The bunkhouse seethed with life for the next fifteen minutes, and a stream of cowboys went rushing out of the long room in a flying file, running toward the barn, toward the corrals, to saddle their horses and ride.

The galloping horses crossed the river, thundering over the wooden bridge, and swerved down the old trail that led in a straighter line toward the canyon where Bat and Loozey held the stolen cattle penned in the brush corral. The men had ridden scarcely five miles on their way, and were ascending a steep slope, walking their horses, when a small man on a brown pony rode into view at the crest of the slope and came rapidly toward them. As he approached he waved an arm.

"Kinney Tavistock!" exclaimed Todd curiously. "What the hell does he want?"

"Oh, he's harmless," chuckled Clink Lafferty. "Maybe he wants to tell you that Yude's got a new batch of moon ready."

Kinney had reached the line of riders now, and he rode up to Karl. Instinctively every man drew rein and turned to watch.

"Mornin', Karl," Kinney greeted with an affable smile on his ugly face. "Let the boys ride on a way, will yuh? I got to see you for a minute."

Karl shot him a hard, penetrating glance, frowned impatiently and turned his head to glance at Todd. "Keep going straight up the trail, Bass," he directed. "I'll join you in a few minutes." He turned his attention back to Kinney, a puzzled, wary look in his blue eyes. "Well, what is it?"

Kinney gestured toward the line of men, again in motion and passing on toward the crest of the slope. "What I got to say ain't for nobody else's ears, Karl. Wait till they git outa hearin' distance."

"Oh, they can't hear what you say." Karl's wariness grew. "Spit it out. We've got a long way to go, and we've got important business to do when we get there. Say what you want to say, and say it quick, or I won't waste time with you."

"They may have important business waitin'," Kinney retorted. "But you got *more* important business at the ranch. Christy's headed that way, to settle accounts with you."

"The hell he is!" Karl's eyes narrowed. "I thought you didn't know him."

"I said I'd never seen him." Kinney gave back his gaze, not at all dashed. "I sent out the word, like you asked. I got word back. He's headed for the Lazy S. Now's your chance to git him. You ain't likely to have another."

Karl turned his head to glance after the men, disappearing over the crest of the slope. He returned his gaze to Kinney's ugly face. "Sounds funny, Kinney. You aren't laying a trap for somebody, are you?"

Kinney gave him a wry, evil grin. "Yeah, I am. For Bark Christy. I know right where he's headed. You go back with me and I'll lead you to him. I got something to settle with that bird. He's been tryin' to make trouble for Yude and me, been tryin' to git us mixed up with his rustlin' schemes. Quicker somebody gets rid of him, the better it'll be for me. No use denyin' it. I ain't leadin' you onto him just because I'm in love with you, yuh know."

"That was my idea," Karl admitted. He glanced again up the slope. The men had ridden quite out of sight. "Damn you, Kinney, this puts me in a jackpot. I've got to lay hands on Bark Christy; and I've got to go with the boys."

"Can't do both," Kinney said flatly. "Gotta decide which is worth most to yuh and do it without wastin' much more time.

Karl cursed in utter exasperation. "I've got to do both. I have to go with the boys—to clean up that little rustling scheme Christy was trying to ring you and Yude in on. So you ought to see the importance of that. But I have to get Bark Christy whether forty rustlers make their escape or not. We'll make for the ranch. But see here, Kinney: if you're lying to me, it's the last lie you'll ever tell. Get that through your thick head! Let's go."

"Fair enough with me." Kinney nudged his brown

pony into step with Dirty. "The boys'll wait for yuh, anyway, when yuh don't show up."

"They'll have to," Karl returned. "They don't know where to go and I couldn't very well direct them. Hit the breeze, Kinney."

They started back to the ranch at a headlong pace, taking advantage of every decent stretch of trail. Karl's brain was working with the precision of an engine. There was something out of line, here, but he could not lay a finger on it. He was morally certain that Kinney *was* mixed up with the rustling scheme, but his remark about going with the Lazy S punchers to surround the rustlers had drawn nothing from Kinney, as he had hoped it might do. Kinney's statement that Christy had tried to involve him and Yude was scarcely warrant for his offering to lead Karl unaware onto Christy. The whole thing savored of some double dealing, and a vague uneasiness took possession of Karl.

On the next upward slope where they were forced to pull their horses down to a walk, Karl addressed Kinney abruptly. "See here, Kinney. This looks queer to me, and I'm half a mind to think you're lying. You'd better come clean and tell me what's what, or I'll turn around and join the boys. What's back of all this, anyhow?"

Kinney surveyed him with opaque yellow eyes. He felt a little inward sweep of dismay. Young Sands was nobody's fool. He'd have to tell him something. Kinney was just shrewd enough to realize that there

214

are times when only one thing will suffice to gain a point, the truth. At least, some of the truth. Besides, what did it matter how much Karl Sands knew? Within another hour he wouldn't be alive to tell it. The opaque yellow eyes lighted with the slow smile that started at Kinney's mouth and spread over his ugly face.

"What proof have I got that if I do come clean, you'll stand by me?"

Karl's gaze held his, boring, intent. "My word, and that's enough. You tell me exactly what's going on, and no matter what you've been up to, I'll keep my mouth shut if you'll play the game with me and help me to land Christy. If that isn't enough for you, we'll have to call a halt. I'm not going on till I know just where you stand, and where I stand."

Kinney's smile faded. His ugly face turned hard. "All right, I'll come clean to the hilt, and if you ever spill what I'm going to tell you, I'll kill you myself! I lied when I said I didn't know Christy. I knew him years ago in Idaho. I got into a rough house there and killed a fellow that damn well needed killing. Christy was in the room and saw it. I got away. After Yude and I set up out here, I thought I was safe. Nobody knew anything about it but Christy, and he was crook enough that he'd never tell unless it stood him to win something by it. See?"

Karl nodded. "I'm beginning to see several things."

Kinney's freckled face twisted in a brutal grin. "You'll see more. Christy drifted out this way and bought the Circle C. He run onto me. He was rustlin' all over the country, and he wanted me to come in as go-between. I told him to go to hell, and he said if I didn't he'd tell on me and get my neck stretched. I was afraid to get in a gun fight with him, so the upshot of it was that I helped him haul the slick ears in. Then the damn fools runs amuck and does that shootin' on your ranch, gits away and comes over to our place and tries to make Yude a tool, too. He and Yude got in a fight. Yude wouldn't believe I'd been rustlin'. Christy knocked Yude out and beat it. Then you come along, and spilled what you knew. I knew damn well you was tellin' the truth. I know Christy. Begin to git the drift?"

Again Karl nodded, and his gaze never left Kinney's face.

"Well, I thought it was time for me to git rid of Christy some way, that's all." Kinney shrugged his indifference to Christy's fate. "You're a crack shot. He is too, but not so good as you are. I just rode over to where I knew I'd find Bark, told him you was on the Lazy S, and got it out of him that he had done the shootin' all right. He said he was goin' over there after you this mornin', and I beat him to it to try to put you wise. On my way in I seen you comin' with the boys, and rode across to catch yuh. It's as much to my interest as it is to yours to git Bark Christy out of the way, only I ain't fool enough to think I could git him. So I'm doin' the next best thing. Satisfied?"

"If you aren't telling the truth, then I never heard it."

Karl's hard gaze traveled slowly over every feature of Kinney's face. "Certainly I'm satisfied. All I wanted to know was what was at the bottom of your actions. I knew you were concerned in that rustling scheme, I'd have bet on it. All right, she goes as she lays. I'll keep my mouth shut, we'll ride in and get the drop on Christy, then you'd better quietly fade out of the country. Some of the other fellows might squeal."

"They can't." Kinney laughed. "Not a damn one knows I'm in it but Christy. There's only two others in it, anyhow. The two you saw in the canyon talking to Bark." He grinned at Karl's start of surprise. "Yeah, I followed you. Let it pass. What do I care what happens to Bat and Loozey? They're worse than Bark. Say, now what the hell!"

They had reached a twist in the trail, and barely a hundred yards ahead and to the right they saw Sheriff Whiteside and a small group of riders coming toward them. Karl tensed in the saddle, his gaze leaping from man to man. Two of them were Ed Martin and Lew Gister. Karl spoke in a low aside to Kinney:

"Keep your hair on and let me do the talking."

In the next few seconds they had come face to face with the group, and everybody drew rein. Karl saw himself confronted by a row of harsh determined faces. The grimmest of all was easily the sheriff himself. He gave Karl one hard look and spoke without preamble.

"Pity you didn't beat it outa the country if you wanted to keep goin'. Played a slick one on me, didn't you? Well, you're played out. Hand over your gun and come peaceable, will you?"

"What's the matter with you, Whitey?" Karl eyed him steadily. "I told you the truth, and in about thirty minutes I'm going to prove it."

Whiteside raised his heavy brows and shrugged. "You ain't provin' nothin'. We been lookin' for you ever since you got out of Sundown, and we're takin' you. Hand over that gun and be quick about it."

Karl sat rigid in the saddle. "I'm not handing over my gun, Whitey. I'm on my way to take Bark Christy, and you nor nobody else is going to stop me, I'm not coming with you to get my neck stretched, while the man you really want is left to slip out of the country. I told you Bark Christy did it, and I can prove it by—"

"You can't prove it by nobody or nothin'," Kinney cut in shrilly. "You can't prove a thing till you git him. I never seen him, but I'm willin' to help you round him up. You gonna sit here and argue with these fools all day?"

Karl felt a wave of chill. No proof in Kinney. Kinney would protect himself to the last. Even in that moment of heat and peril Karl had a fleeting thought that he didn't blame him. Glaring into Whiteside's angry face, Karl raised himself slightly in the stirrups.

"I'm going after Christy. Get out of my way, Whitey! You can follow me, the whole damn bunch of you, and if I'm not telling you the truth, you can take me in and be damned. Get up, Dirty!" The muddy colored horse half reared on his powerful haunches and leaped forward. Kinney's brown pony followed.

Whiteside swung his mount out of the way with a curse. "After him, boys!" he shouted. "Don't let him git outa sight. If he's tellin' the truth, we'll give him a chance to prove it. If he's tryin' to make a slick get-away, he'll never have the chance to make another. After him!

The whole line of nine riders whirled about and swung into a long gallop, in the wake of Karl and Kinney.

Kinney's treacherous brain was working like a trip hammer. Everything was working into his hands. In a little while he would be out of there with his skirts clear. Karl was being led like a lamb to the slaughter. Once Bark had disposed of Karl, the sheriff and his men would shoot Christy down on the spot. There would be no one left who could say a thing against Kinney Tavistock. His face was lighted from within by evil triumph as he followed Karl's horse at a mad pace. Within a quarter mile of the ranch he shouted to Karl to pull up, and rode alongside him.

"Look here," he said smoothly. "We've got to do some quick plannin', Karl?"

"Yes?" Karl snapped out the word with nerve-worn impatience.

"Wait for Whitey and the boys, and leave it to me. We got to go slow, or that damn Christy'll get away from us. Can't make no fool moves this late in the game." He turned to glance back, to where Whiteside and the other eight men were racing toward them a few rods behind.

As the nine men approached and saw the two in the lead evidently waiting for them, they drew down to a trot, to a walk, and stopped. Kinney rode up to Whiteside, Karl hugging close at his horse's flank, and addressed the sheriff confidentially.

"Look here, Whitey, we got to take it easy from here. This Christy told it out that he was comin' to the Lazy S this mornin' to git Karl. Karl and the boys from the ranch had started out to round up the rustlers that's been draggin' a long loop around here. I caught Karl and advised him to come back here and stop Christy. I know just about where Christy's plannin' to hide out, from what this fella said. We all go tearin' in there and Christy's gonna see us and beat it. We got to take it easy."

Whiteside eyed him with a penetrating gaze. "Yeah? Well, what's *your* idea?"

"We'll walk our horses from here on. This side the bridge we'll ditch the horses and go on over the bridge afoot. Once we're across the bridge, you fellas sneak along in the cottonwoods by the river. You stay cached there till we run this Christy out. Otherwise we ain't gonna git him."

"Well, that's reasonable," Whiteside admitted. "All right, go ahead. But if you try playin' any tricks, Tavistock, you'll be a damn sorry man. It ain't goin' to take long to see whether you're tellin' the truth or not. Get on with you."

The small troup of riders rode on at a walk, keeping to cover, careful not to expose themselves where they would be seen from the ranch buildings. When they reached the bridge, they left their horses in a herd, tethered in a thick grove of cottonwoods. Walking lightly, the eleven men crossed the bridge, Karl and Kinney in the lead. Having crossed the river, they left the bridge behind, and the sheriff with his posse disappeared as silently as shadows into the cottonwoods along the bank.

Karl and Kinney went down the road toward the house. As they approached the ranch house, Karl drew a breath of relief. "Whew! I was afraid Whitey would insist on snaking right along with us. God, Kinney! You'd better be telling the truth!"

The moment Karl's back was turned, Kinney shot a scrutinizing look over the flat. No one would have dreamed that the sheriff and a posse of eight men was hidden in the cottonwoods. The ranch seemed to be utterly deserted for the time. Kinney's gaze riveted on the barn and the adjacent corrals. He was the living embodiment of treachery. He would play square with Christy for two reasons. One, he was afraid of Christy, he dared not make the least slip in leading Karl Sands to certain death: the other, he knew that was one sure way to put Christy beyond the power of telling what he knew, to make sure that Christy got Karl so that Whiteside and the men would get Christy. He stared intently at the barn and corrals, and raised one hand as if he would brush back his hair.

Anyone seeing the gesture could think nothing of it, at least not anyone save Barker Christy. It was a pre-arranged signal with Christy, signifying that Kinney was there with Karl, that Christy was to keep his eyes open and be ready. Behind the big corral, the pole corral next the barn, quite hidden by the barn from the cottonwoods and the men hidden among them, there was a slight gleam of white for a moment. Christy's hand. Another prearranged signal. Christy was there, waiting. Kinney hid a small smile, and tined Karl as Karl turned, beckoned to him, ducked his head to prevent his being seen through the window, and slipped past the house.

"We got to find out the time," Kinney whispered. "I planned this thing with an eye to makin' no slips. I know just when he'll be there."

Karl made no answer. He felt a surge of repulsion for the small ugly man at his side, for any man who could so coolly plot the death of another. Come to think of it, Kinney wasn't a great deal better than Christy. Only, this time, he was playing into the hands of justice. The only thing to do was to make the best of it, get the drop on Christy, and pray that Kinney would get his needings sometime somewhere. The two men hurried on to the bunkhouse, and went into the room to look at the big tin alarm clock on the shelf just inside the door.

"Ten minutes till six," Karl read the stained dial.

Kinney swore a disgruntled oath. "Damn the luck! Ain't no use goin' up there yet. He won't show up till around seven. You got anything around here to eat? I ain't had my breakfast, and I'm hungry as hell."

"Why yes, I suppose you can get something in the cookshack," Karl answered, impatient at the delay. "Where the hell is he heading for, anyway?"

"One of them draws up there by the horse pasture," Kinney said. "He's intendin' to leave his mount there and sneak down. He'll git there a few minutes before seven, and we'll git there a few minutes before he does. But we gotta kill a little time. Let's go over to the cookshack."

They walked across the intervening few yards of ground to the small building where Soupy Groggs did his cooking and fed the men. Karl poked around among Soupy's pots and boxes and brought out some bread and beans, some cold fried potatoes and a few strips of leftover bacon. Kinney ate standing, with enough of voracity to back up the bluff of his hunger, while Karl paced the floor restlessly. Having eaten all he could hold, Kinney suggested that they go out into the yard and walk around.

"I guess I'm kinda on my nerve," he confessed. "This waitin' around ain't my dish. Don't it give yuh the jim jams, though?"

"Well, I'd as soon have it over with," Karl laughed shortly. "But it doesn't do any good to let it get on your nerves."

They went out of the cookshack and Kinney's gaze turned indolently upon the big corral. He could see a dark blur at one place where the barn wall showed through the poles. He knew it for the crouching, waiting Christy. Anyone not knowing the man was there, not looking closely to locate him, would never have the least suspicion of his presence. Kinney shot a sidelong glance at the restless, preoccupied Karl. Sheep to the slaughter was right, and no exaggeration. In a very few minutes this man who walked beside him would be lying dead on the ground. And the man behind the corral would be dead, too. He would leap and run to make his escape, and the sheriff would do the rest. A warning shout from him, Kinney, would ascertain that.

Kinney recast swiftly the arrangements made between him and Christy. It was all very simple, really. For Christy to come to the ranch when every hand was out on the hunt for the rustlers: for Kinney to intercept Karl and bring him back: for Kinney to get Karl's gun away from him and lead him up to the spot where Christy lay in waiting. All very simple. The next thing was to get Karl's gun, so that he could make no use of that deadly aim of his. A reasonable ruse, Kinney mused. What would be a reasonable ruse? He thought intently for a moment as they strolled aimlessly about the yard, before one came to him. Then again he hid that small treacherous smile, paused and yawned.

"How the hell did you ever git to be such a crack shot, Karl?" he asked, tone and words the essence of guile. Any man would have taken them for the chance remark impelled by a wandering curiosity.

"Practice," said Karl shortly.

"Yeah!" Kinney laughed. "I practiced a lot too, but I never got to be no crack shot at it."

Karl shrugged, little interested in the conversation and in the subject of target practice. "Oh, well, some men naturally take to shooting. I guess I did. That's one reason I always pack a thirty-eight, lighter gun, better for fine shooting."

Kinney chuckled. "Yeah, I guess that's what Christy thought. He went and bought a thirty-eight, but it didn't do much good. Yude took it away from him, so he had to go back to packin' the old forty-four. I always like a good big bore, myself. But I can't do much with a gun. I bet you I couldn't even hit a can on that corral fence, from as close as fifty feet."

"What?" Karl turned upon him a surprised glance, his wandering and preoccupied attention caught for a moment. "Hell, any man could do that."

Kinney grinned, and the grin was underlaid by quivering triumph. The ruse was working. "Yuh think so, do yuh? All right, I'll show you. Wait till I git a can." He went back to the cookshack, while Karl stood waiting for him with a half-impatient half-amused smile on his somber young face. He returned with an empty tomato can, taken from the heap Soupy had piled by the door.

He knew that he must move with precision now, in everything he did. It would take little to rouse Karl's suspicions. If he was to rid the world in the next few moments of the two men who could do him harm, he must make no slips. He must impress Karl Sands with the idea that he was momentarily interested in the business of a little target practice, and prevent any least doubt from arising as to the sincerity of his motives.

Karl watched him, as he went to fetch the can, wondering how any man could find room in his brain for the silly entertainment of target practice when a momentous issue was to be at stake in the next half or three-quarters of an hour. Well, there was no accounting for men, and the quirks of their minds. Kinney was something of a child, for all his shrewdness. He was betraying a child's capacity for fixing upon trivial things to fill up a gap when his nerves were unstrung. Might as well humor him, since there wasn't anything else to do right now.

Inside the house, Jeudi had gone into the kitchen to start a fire and get Frank's breakfast. As she had done every morning since she had lived in the John Day country, she walked to the outer door to look upon the majesty of the breaks, for the breaks were visible from Sundown, and she had felt a glow of gratitude that they proved visible also from the ranch. She opened the kitchen door and stepped out upon the porch, her eyes raised to the sky line where the rock ribbed mountains rose to greet the sun. But before she quite brought her line of vision to the breaks, she saw Karl and Kinney Tavistock walking across the yard toward the corral. She frowned, wondering what their presence could mean, hesitated a moment, then whirled, ran across the kitchen and into the living room to tell her father.

"Father!" She was breathless as she paused before him. "Karl's out in the yard!"

Sands rose instinctively to his feet, his bandaged face going blank with astonishment. "Karl is!"

"Yes. And that ugly little Tavistock twin is with him." Jeudi frowned, startled by the sight of the two men she had not expected to see, uneasy, with a premonition that all was not as it should be suddenly assailing her. "What are they doing there? Why do you suppose Karl has come back?"

"That's what I was asking myself, Judy." Sands bit his lip and shook his head. "I don't believe I like it."

"I'm going to stay right there at the kitchen window and see just what's going on," Jeudi assured him. "After what Karl said about going after Christy—it looks so *queer*."

"It does," agreed Sands. "I knew long ago, Judy, that something pretty bad was going to happen. But there's been enough! My God, child, does there have to be more bloodshed before this mess is settled?"

Jeudi shrank. "Oh! Don't say it! Don't even think it! It mustn't be. I'm going out into the kitchen and see what they're doing."

Sands heard the swift light sound of her footsteps as she went from the room. She attained her vantage point at the window, only to see that Karl and Kinney were still walking slowly toward the corral. Kinney was talking, but his words did not carry to her ears, only the faintly audible sound of his voice.

The cottonwoods by the river were much nearer to the corrals than the house. The sheriff and his men could hear clearly the words being said between Karl and Kinney Tavistock. Whiteside scowled, taking in all the byplay with intent eyes. As Kinney came from the cookshack carrying the empty can, the sheriff spoke to Lew Gister in a low undertone.

"Now what the hell are they pullin' that stunt for? Shootin' at a can to kill time! Looks phony to me, Giss."

"Well, it does look kind of funny," Gister admitted. "What the hell do they want to kill time for?"

"One too many for me," Whiteside grunted, chewing at his mustache. "I thought they was so hell bent to get a hold of Christy. You suppose they're tryin' some smart trick to give us the slip?"

"You know, I don't think they are," Ed Martin put in, from his position at Whiteside's right elbow. "Look at Karl. He's sorta het up about something, and I'll bet a hat this stallin' around is Kinney's doing. He's talkin' kind of big, if you'll notice. What the hell's he so interested in showin' Karl how rotten a shot he is for, anyway?"

Whiteside was watching Kinney intently, missing no least move the little man was making. "He's just killin' time, for some reason, I tell yuh," the sheriff insisted. "That's what he pretends to be doin', and for once in his life he's tellin' the truth, if he never tells it again. He's killin' time, all right—but I gotta hunch that he ain't killin' it for the reason he wants us to think he is. Keep your eye on that bird. Look at him!"

"So you think any man could hit a can like that from fifty feet, do yuh?" Kinney was saying, balancing the can on his hand. "Well, I maybe might hit it once out of four shots. I doubt it." He cocked a speculative eye at the gun in Karl's holster. "Might do better if I had your gun, you say them thirty-eights is better, bein' lighter, for fine shootin'. Can I try it with your gun?"

Whiteside, under cover of the cottonwoods by the river, scowled and muttered a round oath. "Now what does he mean by that move? What's he tryin' to do, damn him! Git Karl unarmed?"

"Looks like it," Ed Martin answered, beset by a sudden uneasiness. "Damn it, Whitey, I don't like this business. There's something crooked about the whole proceeding."

"You ain't tellin' me anything," snapped Whiteside. "Shut up and keep your eye on Kinney, will yuh?"

Martin did not retort that Whiteside had spoken first, he diplomatically relapsed into silence, and the group of men hidden in the trees breathed softly, that not a word spoken between the two men on the flat a few yards away should escape them.

When Kinney asked to try the target shooting with Karl's gun, Karl looked at him queerly, and for the first time it struck him that Kinney was acting like a man with a settled intent. But Kinney wasn't going to try anything crooked with the sheriff and eight other men looking on. Whatever Kinney was up to, Karl had

229

a strong curiosity to determine. He drew his thirty-eight from his holster, deliberately broke it open and ejected the cartridges from the cylinder. Then he closed the gun and handed it to Tavistock, who stood watching him with an expressionless face.

"I don't know that I'm trusting you too damn far, Kinney," he said, giving the ugly little man a straight look. "You may have the gun—empty, till you get that can set up."

Kinney laughed. "Hell! You think I'm pullin' some crazy stunt? You think I ain't got a gun because you don't see it?" He flipped back his loose coat, and revealed the butt of a gun thrust into his trouser waist-band. He laughed again. But, cripes! That's all right. I don't blame yuh for bein' suspicious of everybody. Wait till I put this can up. Hell! I didn't know you carried a Smith & Wesson."

Karl raised his eyebrows in some slight surprise. "Does it matter? I happen to like the action, that's all."

Kinney shrugged. "I just reckoned you'd carry a Colt like everybody else does. Why would it matter? Well, I said I was gonna put this can up. I better do it, or we won't have any time for target practice. We got to be gittin' outa here before long."

He walked toward the corral, ostentatiously turning the Smith & Wesson gun over in his hand, seemingly with very admiring eyes. Karl strolled slowly behind him, dropping the six cartridges into his pocket, sharply watching Kinney's every move. What was the man up to? He was up to something, and a little target shooting was not the whole of it.

Kinney walked straight toward the part of the corral where Christy crouched hidden behind the fence. With a last look at the gun, the little man made a show of laying it on the top pole of the corral fence. He did it in such a way that he knew the gun would fall to the ground. Here he was quite hidden from the sight of the men in the cottonwoods. With his back to Karl, he laid the gun on the fence, and with an almost soundless undertone he spoke to Christy.

"Here's his gun. Empty."

" 'S all right," muttered Christy. "I got three shells that'll fit it—if I need a second gun. Beat it."

"Wait till you hear me say 'I forgot,'" Kinney ordered. "That's your cue."

He turned and looked back at Karl. "I guess I better put it along this way more," he decided, calling to Karl and squinting along the fence. "Too dark there." He walked along the fence to place the can in position, and as he did so he unobtrusively jarred the top pole. The carefully balanced Smith & Wesson thirty-eight fell to the ground within a few inches of Christy's hand. Christy reached into his pocket, drew out the three thirty-eight shells he had dropped there the day before, and had the gun loaded before Kinney had gone twenty feet. He might have to use a second gun. Never could tell. Better always be ready.

Very carefully he placed the three shells in the cylinder, to the left, leaving the three empty chambers to the right, so that at the first pull of the trigger the cylinder would roll and place the first of the three shells in the firing chamber directly under the dog.

Kinney was just setting the can on the top pole. He rejoined Karl with the mildly excited air of a child about to engage a new toy.

"There she is, all ready to plunk," he stated with a cheerfulness that took all his effort to achieve. So near the completion of his plans now. He must not make a slip. His throat was dry with excitement. His brain wanted to whirl, but he set his teeth doggedly against it. "Of course, you can hit 'er there, all right."

In the cottonwoods by the river, Whiteside was growing more suspicious with every passing minute. He nudged Ed Martin, never once taking his eyes from Kinney. "Damn him, what's he doing? What did he do with Karl's gun?"

Before the words were well spoken, he learned what Kinney had done with the gun. Karl spoke, coldly, within a foot of Kinney—but his eyes were riveted on the poles of the corral where Kinney had laid his gun.

"You left my gun back there, Kinney," he said. "It fell down."

Kinney turned his head with a look of amazement. "Hell! Ain't I the dumb one!" Fairly shivering with excitement, striving to hold himself in check that Karl might not read anything of the turmoil going on within him, he spoke the words that gave Barker Christy his cue. "Damn me for a plumb idiot. *I—forgot—*your gun."

232

But Karl Sands had stood like a man turned to wood, his penetrating blue eyes fixed on that spot where the gun had fallen. He saw movement there. He saw a hand reach to pick up the gun. His focused gaze found the blot of shadow that was a man hiding there, and he knew who the man was. In that instant, in one flash, he saw the meaning of the whole proceeding, of Kinney's actions, of Kinney's intent. Kinney, the treacherous, working with Bark Christy. Kinney, who forgot also to give Karl Sands credit for having some intelligence and wit of his own. Karl's swift fury mounted within him, as he made out clearly, now that he was looking for it, the hand of a man, holding a gun pointed directly toward him. He saw it in the same instant that Kinney said *"I—forgot—"*

By the very emphasis and intonation of those words he knew them for a signal, and he leaped. He leaped to the right, toward Kinney. The gun behind the corral roared as he leaped, and a bullet sung past his head. He struck Kinney a violent blow that dashed the small man flat to the ground. His right hand, swift as a striking snake, darted to Kinney's waistband and whipped out the forty-five Colt thrust there. He flattened to his belly as he rolled from Kinney, and his eye leaped unerringly to that spot where he could still see the gun behind the corral, could see it even more clearly from his position on the ground, gripped in Christy's hand.

He raised Kinney's gun, and the uncanny accuracy that had made Karl Sands' name a byword in the John

Day, where fine shooting was concerned, came into play. He shot, not at the man behind the corral, but at the gun in that man's hand. What could the thirty-eight Smith & Wesson profit him—empty? Karl remembered that Yude had taken the thirty-eight Colt away from Christy. The gun that had spat at Karl was a forty-four.

Kinney was up in a flash, and leaped upon Karl with the savagery of a panther. He wrested the gun from Karl's hand, by the foul trick of stamping upon Karl's wrist, numbing the hand for an instant, forcing it to loose its hold. He snatched the gun and threw it as far as his strength would permit, which was far enough away to put it out of all reach so far as Karl was concerned.

But the one bullet Karl had fired had done its work, had done what he had intended it to do. It had struck Christy's forty-four fairly, jamming the gun and putting it hopelessly out of commission. Christy threw it from him with a curse, and snatched up the thirty-eight Smith & Wesson, rising to his feet with a shout of triumph.

"Damn you, I got you now!" He gloated, savoring the relish of the jest. "I've got you, with your own gun. You didn't do so much knockin' my gun out of commission. I had three thirty-eight shells in my pocket. They're as good in this as in a thirty-eight Colt! I sure as hell have got you!"

Karl, white as paper, his blue eyes sparking the fire of his fury, kicked Kinney from him, and leaped to his feet.

Down in the cottonwoods, Whiteside groaned in swift realization. The thing had happened in a split second, almost before a man could draw a breath. Like Karl, he saw through the whole proceeding in a flash of enlightenment. But he saw too late.

"My God, boys!" he cried to the men grouped around him. "Karl was tellin' the truth. That's Christy. I know his voice. But he's got him. None of us can git a line on Christy. Hell and blazes! What's that crazy fool up to?"

For in the same instant that he had leaped to his feet, Karl had started running toward Christy, with long lunging strides. Christy laughed, pointed the unwavering gun at Karl's chest, and pulled the trigger. The gun clicked.

"Oh Gawd," groaned Kinney, from all fours, where he crouched watching, helpless, paralyzed by fear and consternation. "My *Gawd!* Old shells—missed fire!"

From the porch of the house a scream cut the air. Jeudi had seen the lightning movement of events. She cried out as Karl knocked Kinney flat and snatched his gun from him, cried out in panic and started running toward the door.

"Father! Oh, God, Father!"

Sands leaped to his feet and came rushing blindly into the kitchen as she darted out the door, and her added words struck his ears and flooded him with horror.

"Father! They're trying to kill Karl!"

He, blundering blindly, reached the door as she

reached the porch steps. "What?" he cried harshly. "Who? Judy! What's going on out there?" Somebody trying to kill Karl. Sands groaned aloud in his welter of fear and shock. "God, if I could only see!" He tore the bandage from his face, lifting the mutilated sightless countenance, and the prayer that poured from his lips was a prayer from hell. "God, if there is a God anywhere, give me my sight!" The prayer raised to a cry. "Give me my sight!"

But the light that fell upon his face did not penetrate to his scarred eyeballs. And Jeudi screamed. She screamed as Karl went lunging toward Christy, as Christy pulled trigger and the gun missed fire.

A look of blank astonishment crossed Christy's face. But no fear. One shell might miss fire, but the other two couldn't. They couldn't all be bad. They weren't so old. Karl was coming nearer in great leaps, a perfect target. Gloating, Christy pulled the trigger again. The hammer raised, the cylinder rolled, and the hammer fell. The gun clicked.

"Gawd! Gawd!" Kinney was whimpering now. "Why don't the fool buy decent shells! Another missed fire!"

The sheriff and his men broke from the cover of the cottonwoods, as Karl started toward Christy and passed from their view. They came running in mad excitement, every man with his weapon out and ready to fire.

Christy licked his lips. Fear rode him now. But the next one had to be good. Two could miss fire, not three! Karl was almost upon him. Karl was not three feet away when Christy pulled the trigger the third time. The third time the hammer rolled and fell, the third time the gun clicked. In the next instant the gun was wrested from his hand, and Karl Sands had him by the throat.

With a wild cry, Jeudi leaped down the steps and went running toward the gathering men. Whiteside and his posse were drawing close to the two struggling by the corral. From the bridge came the thunder of galloping horses' hoofs. The line of riders, hidden by the cottonwoods, were racing toward the flat at head-long speed. Then the riders swung into sight beyond the thick cottonwoods, clattering down the road in a cloud of dust.

Karl, oblivious to everything else, had Christy by the throat, and he had all his raging heart demanded of life. He had justification and vindication within his grasp. He wrested the gun from Christy's grasp and shoved it into his holster with his left hand, even as his right hand closed on Christy's throat and bore the man backward. Christy's finely built body was all muscle, and he struggled desperately.

Karl crashed a furious fist on his jaw, making his brain reel, half crazing him with pain. He tried to strike back, but Karl's fist descended again. Blow after blow battered in Christy's face, about his head, till he reeled and drooped in Karl's grip. Within a very few minutes, Christy was bruised and battered to submission, too groggy and belabored to make any move toward defense.

Kinney had struggled to his knees, to his feet, and had gone on a shambling run toward the gun he had cast from Karl's grasp. He literally fell upon it, got drunkenly to his feet, and brought the gun up to an aim at Karl's back. He brought it up with the swiftness and deftness of a man who knew how to use guns, and use them well.

Whiteside's Colt roared righteous anger and retribution. Kinney half whirled about, a foolish look on his ugly face, a bullet in his brain, crashed to the ground and lay kicking like a beheaded chicken.

"That's the last time you'll ever try to lead a man into a death trap," the sheriff shouted to ears that would hear no more, as he came rushing on.

Karl turned about, panting from exertion, holding Christy tightly in his grasp. His eyes were ablaze with triumph, like blue fires. His blond face was white with excitement. Some of the lines were erased from it. He saw collected there to face him the sheriff and the posse, the crew of the Lazy S, and Jeudi, and his father, gripping Jeudi's hand, wrung in an agony of suspense. Karl looked from face to face, then he turned to the battered Christy, cowering and twisting in his grip.

"You've got whom?" Karl's voice was the essence of irony. "You're the one who's got, Christy." Sands cried out in relief at the sound of his son's voice. Karl went on heedlessly. "Why did you shoot at my father, damn you? Tell! Tell Whiteside, tell everybody. Quick, before I let you have it again."

"I didn't mean to shoot him!" Christy, cowed, was Christy the coward. "I thought he was you. You got to give me a chance. You got to give me a trial."

"Sure, we'll give him a trial!" Whiteside laughed, a sound that made Christy shiver. "Right here and now. I'm judge and jury. Go ahead and finish him, Karl, if it'll do you any good."

Karl smiled. "Thanks, Whitey. I get you. But you know what he hates more than anything in the world? He hates the thought of having his neck stretched. There's plenty of rope lying around. Take mine, off Dirty. But bury it with him. I'd hate to think of ever using it on a decent cow again. There. Take him."

With a violent shove, he sent Christy sprawling headlong at their feet. Half a dozen men fell upon the killer.

"Come in the house, boy," Sands said hoarsely. "You don't really want to see this. Come in the house, and get your breath."

"I can't." Karl looked up at the faces of the Lazy S cowboys. Soupy Groggs was crying openly, the tears running down his lantern-jawed face, unashamed. The other men were shifting on their feet, looking at him and away, and Riceman held his head down. Karl laughed. "You know what I told you before I 'gave myself up,' Clink? I meant that. Would you kindly tell the other boys what it was."

"I already told 'em." Lafferty mumbled the words, flushing.

"Damn it, man!" the sheriff blurted. "Of all the sheer

grit! You runnin' onto Christy in the face of that gun. But it was a fool's chance you took. What if them three shells had been good?"

Karl smiled, then laughed aloud, and drew the gun from his holster. "Not so much of a chance as you think, Whitey. When he said he had three shells, I knew how he'd place them. I just banked on his not knowing what every man doesn't know. See?" He held up the gun. "A Colt cylinder rolls to the right. This Smith & Wesson Special rolls to the left. It rolled the cartridges *away* from the firing chamber. All I had to do was get him before it rolled clear around to the shells. Hell, the shells are all right."

He aimed at the can Kinney had placed upon the fence. He pulled the trigger and the hammer rose, the cylinder rolled to the left. The hammer fell. The gun spat lead and the can bounced from the corral pole.

Whiteside gaped. "I'll be damned."

"We'll all be damning ourselves," Karl returned crisply, "if we don't get out of here in jig time and ride down those rustlers. We've lost a good hour."

"You go after 'em, you and the boys," Whiteside answered, imperturbably. He glanced with significant eyes at the despairing Christy, now bound and tied to the back of a horse. "I got a job to attend to already. You really want me to take your rope?"

"I do." A queer expression glowed deep in Karl's eyes. "I'd just like to contribute to the cause. He nearly made a mess of things for me. I'd like to send him to hell on my rope. I'll get another from the barn."

The murmur of men's voices, in at least twenty different species of excited comment, rose in the yard as he turned and strode toward the barn. Men and horses milled, around Christy, around the sheriff. Whiteside took his posse and set off toward the bridge, beyond which their horses were waiting. The Lazy S boys, all but Bert Gray (who went with Whiteside to get a horse in return for the one he had lent as carrier to Christy), mounted their horses, and sat talking rather furiously as they waited for Karl.

He came out quickly, a coiled rope slung over his arm, and stopped before his father. "You and Judy go in and take it easy, Frank. I have to go. I'm the only one who knows where to go. You take good care of him till I get back, Judy. When I get far enough that I can show the boys where to pick up the men and the cattle, I'll come back as fast as I can get here. We'll make time in the daylight. I ought to get here by sundown. You remember what I said, Judy? Till—then!"

He beckoned to the waiting men and started down the road at a long stride. "I have to walk as far as across the bridge, boys. Dirty's tied over there, waiting for me. Fan 'em on the tail! We're off."

Jeudi stood holding her father's hand, motionless, watching till the group had passed from sight beyond the cottonwoods. "There. They're gone." She gripped Sands' hand tightly. "We might as well go in. You know—no, of course you don't know. Come on in the house and I'll tell you everything that happened." They went across the yard arm in arm, into the house, and came to pause in the living room, both of them forgetting the breakfast Jeudi had been going to prepare.

Jeudi dropped into a chair, but Sands paced the floor, excited, still bewildered and unable to understand just what had happened, only that Karl had proved himself, that Christy had been taken.

"You—you were going to tell me," he reminded, and Jeudi roused from her reverie.

"I don't know everything that happened. We'll have to wait till Karl comes back to get to the bottom of it. Only, he and Kinney came here for something, and Christy was hidden out there. Kinney tried to double-cross Karl, but Karl got the best of them and the sheriff shot Kinney. He and the posse took Kinney's body away with them, when they went to—to hang Christy. The first I saw,—" And she gave him the full account of all she knew, with minute attention to detail, with infinite patience. "I think Kinney must have brought him here, planning treachery from the first."

"There's no other answer," Sands replied. "When Karl gets back we'll know. He said he'd get back by sundown, didn't he?"

"By sundown," said Jeudi.

In the town of Sundown, In Parkin's Place, the world was out of joint. Dutch wandered about like a lost dog, his little green eyes an empty sea of distress. Jeudi was gone. Nothing would ever be the same, with Jeudi

242

gone. The early morning light that lay upon the breaks had glory no more. Jeudi was gone. Dutch walked heavily to the front of the saloon, and stood staring into the street. A man came riding across the bridge, across the John Day river, riding in haste, on some urgent errand. He rode down the street and approached the saloon, and Dutch saw that he was one of the cowboys from the Bar C Bar.

"Hello, Dutch!" The cowboy drew rein, and he had the air of a man bearing very important news.

"H'lo, Amby," Dutch returned, with heavy courtesy. "What you doin' in town this early?"

"Oh, damn it, I got to go to Heppner. Had to come by here to get some money the boss wanted me to pick up."

"You don't like it to go to Heppner, no?" Dutch's green eyes gazed at him, unseeing. "Oh, it ain't such a bad trip yet."

"Hell," Amby protested, "I don't mind going to Heppner. I just hated to be cut out of the fun when the manhunt's gettin' hot. Sheriff's workin' up that way with a posse. Karl Sands was seen up there in the hills. Got the word from one of the moonshiners, he told us. They're after him like hell a beatin' tanbark."

Dutch's green eyes focused on Amby's face, and there was interest in them enough now. "What's that you say? They going to git Karl, yet?"

"Sure are!" Amby verified, with the positiveness of a man who knows. "Well, I might as well git along."

Parkin gazed after the departing horseman, his big

body tensed and drawn to full height. They were after Karl! Jeudi ought to know about that. Karl hadn't kept himself under cover. He had been seen, and they were going to get him. Parkin turned back into his Place. The grays were fast. Somebody ought to be there with Jeudi, somebody like him, who had known her always, who could hold her steady when the world crashed. The grays were very fast. He could get there by sundown.

The sun was dipping behind the breaks when Karl rode across the bridge that spanned the river, on the road that led to home. He passed the cottonwoods fringing the river, and came out into the flat. Peace lay like a pearl silk veil over everything. He had the impulse to walk softly. He removed his riding gear from Dirty, and turned the horse loose onto the feeding flat. He stood for a moment, his eyes upon the far majestic breaks, where the red rock ribs of the mountains glowed in the last light of the sun. He crossed the yard and went into the house.

He entered the living room, and came to a halt just inside the door. In the last gold light of the day three people sat there waiting for him. Jeudi, with her black eyes clinging to his face the moment he appeared. Frank, sitting tense, upright in his chair, his sightless face turned toward the door. And beyond Frank, Dutch: huge lumbering Dutch, rocking back and forth, utterly unable to sit still. Here too peace lay, waiting. And Karl, searching for some word, thought only of what he had said to Jeudi.

"Well—it's sundown."

Dutch supplied the missing key to speech: too excited and pleased with life to search for the right thing to say, he said it.

"It ain't sundown for none of us no more, yet. It's sunrise."

Eli(za) Colter was born in Portland, Oregon. At the age of thirteen she was afflicted for a time by blindness, an experience that taught her to "drill out" her own education for the remainder of her life. Although her first story was published under a *nom de plume* in 1918, she felt her career as a professional really began when she sold her first story to *Black Mask Magazine* in 1922. Her style clearly indicates a penchant for what is termed the "hard-boiled school" in stories that display a gritty, tough, violent world. Sometimes there are episodes that become littered with bodies. Over the course of a career that spanned nearly four decades, Colter wrote more than 300 stories and serials, mostly Western fiction. She appeared regularly in thirty-seven different magazines, including slick publications like *Liberty*, and was showcased on the covers of Fiction House's *Lariat Story Magazine* along with the like of Walt Coburn. She published seven hardcover Western novels. Colter was particularly adept at crafting complex and intricate plots set against traditional Western storylines of her day—range wars, cattlemen vs. homesteaders, and switched identities. Yet, no matter what the plot, she somehow always managed to include the unexpected and unconventional, as she did in her best novels, such as *Outcast of Lazy S* (1933) or *Cañon Rattlers* (1939).

Center Point Publishing
600 Brooks Road ● PO Box 1
Thorndike ME 04986-0001 USA

(207) 568-3717

US & Canada:
1 800 929-9108
www.centerpointlargeprint.com